D1569509

Scan the QR code
to see what others
have to say about
this book.

N/A

# CHAPPIE AND ME

# CHAPPIE AND ME

## An Autobiographical Novel

### by John Craig

DODD, MEAD & COMPANY · NEW YORK

1 2 3 4 5 6 7 8 9 10

Library of Congress Cataloging in Publication Data
Craig, John, 1921–
    Chappie and me.
I. Title.
PZ4.C8858Ch 1979     [PR9199.3.c68]     813'.5'4     79–664
ISBN 0-396-07660-2

In essence, this is a true story. I
know because I was there.

But it is told under the novelist's
license to shape time and place to
his purpose. Let it be the more
real for that.

In any event, there *was* a barn-
storming black baseball team
called the Colored All Stars.

And there certainly was a Chappie Johnson.

This book is for him.

# *I*

That summer, as every other of my boyhood, Chappie Johnson brought his Colored All Stars to town to play against our Trentville Trents.

I remember that particular visit as if it were yesterday.

The evening of the game we had supper, as usual, in the big kitchen of the house we rented, a block off the main street at the north end of town. I don't suppose my mother thought so as she worked over the wood stove, but it always seemed to me to be cool in that kitchen, even on days when the burning sun turned the asphalt of the streets into spongy gumbo under your bare feet. The table was covered with rose-patterned oil cloth, and on the side by the window there was a permanent cluster of salt and pepper shakers, catsup bottle, covered sugar bowl, and a sealer of homemade sweet pepper relish. I even know what we had to eat—potato soup, which was one of my dad's favorites, and creamed salmon on toast, which certainly wasn't one of mine.

Like Christmas, the start of deer hunting, and the opening of the Trentville Agricultural Exhibition, the annual appearance of the All Stars was an important date on the calendar of our town.

That was a dozen or so years before Jackie Robinson and Branch Rickey finally broke through organized baseball's color barrier. Most of the best blacks—Josh Gibson, Cool Papa Bell, Satchell Paige—were playing with teams like the Kansas City Monarchs, Homestead Grays and Pittsburg Crawfords in the Negro National and American Leagues. The very next summer Paige would out-pitch Dizzy Dean, a 30-game winner that year, in an exhibition game and beat the St. Louis Cards 1–0 in 13 innings. And Gibson would hit a ball clear out of Yankee Stadium, something nobody else ever did—not Ruth or Gehrig or DiMaggio or Mantle or Maris.

In Trentville we didn't know anything about any of that—not even my dad, who had the *St. Louis Sporting News*, baseball's bible, mailed to him every week.

We did realize that Chappie had some great ballplayers on his touring club, though we had no way of comprehending that they included the Henry Aarons, Frank Robinsons and Vida Blues of their day. You won't find their names in the record books, but they could do it all, you can believe that. All and more, because they had to entertain too. Be clowns, fools, wandering court jesters. Astound. Do tricks. Perform feats of magic. Jig around. Be loose. Dance the cakewalk. Have rhythm. Make us laugh until our sides ached at how funny they were. Make us shake our heads in wonderment at how good they were.

2

I don't think there was any real prejudice against Negroes in our little Ontario city, mainly because we hardly ever met up with any. There wasn't one among our 24,569 residents, and you could walk the main street every day without once looking into a black face. Our view of them was based on *Uncle Tom's Cabin*, church minstrel shows, Amos 'n Andy on radio ("I'se regusted, Madam Queen"), and Stepinfetchit in the movies.

When Chappie's posters appeared around town, we said "Hey, the niggers are comin' back," or "Them 'coons sure put on a show." Even my father, very much a liberal for his time and place, could do no better than "darkies."

It simply never occurred to us that they might resent such names; it was just what they were called. Oh, we were capable of racism, all right—the Indians around town could have told you all about that. But, where Chappie and his ballplayers were concerned, what we had was a ton of ignorance.

To come right down to it, if they made us uncomfortable, it was because we were more than a little intimidated by them. They came from places none of us had ever been to, places from an outside world with names that sounded far away and romantic, and somehow superior—Montgomery, Alabama . . . Memphis, Tennessee . . . Little Rock, Arkansas. They seemed to get more kick out of life than we did, to see a funny side to it that was beyond us, to laugh at things we couldn't understand.

Anyway, everybody in town said Chappie's players were good boys. Always showed up on time, always gave you your money's worth. Never caused any trouble. Knew their place. Not uppity. And always gone within an hour of the final out.

Baseball was still mostly a day game then. Some of the big league parks had lights, so did Toronto's Triple 'A' Maple Leaf Stadium. But, in places like Trentville, the prospect of seeing a night game was an extra gate attraction. The All Stars brought their own lighting equipment—a gasoline-powered generator, a couple of hundred yards of worn, frayed cable, and a dozen or so standards, about as high as a tall stepladder, which supported small banks of 100-watt light bulbs. The "towers" were made of iron pipe, badly rusted, and came in sections that could be bolted together or taken down in a few minutes. They groaned and swayed when it was windy. The lighting system was transported from town to town in a wheezing, 10-ton truck that was of about the same vintage as the old, beat-up bus that carried the players.

I was a couple of months shy of my 16th birthday that July evening in 1933.

My dad always liked to get to the ball park long before the plate umpire called "Play ball!" to start the game. He would pretend that it was part of his duties as official scorer, for which he got two bucks a game; but we both knew that he just wanted to be part of that magic time, that special, relaxed time, before the fans started to fill up the stands, and you hear the crack of bat on ball, and the easy, yippy chatter of the players, and nobody has struck out with runners in scoring position or messed up a routine double play. He'd stand around, a familiar part of it, talking and joking; and then, about five minutes before game time, he'd go into the ramshackle press box, next to the home team dugout, with the chicken wire sagging across the front of it, and print the starting line-ups in his score book with a thick, yellow soft-lead pencil.

It was probably about a quarter to seven when we left the house to trace the familiar route to the ball park. Hot and oppressive, without the trace of a breeze to rustle the leaves. The giant thermometer in front of the *Examiner* where my dad was an editor had reached 87 degrees that afternoon, and there were some thunderheads forming in the west. I was silently praying that the rain would hold off; it would be a long twelve months before the All Stars came our way again.

Trentville had been hard hit by the Great Depression. A third of the men were out of work, and a great many families were on relief. The NO HELP WANTED sign in the employment office of the bridge-side mill was stained and sun-bleached, and looked as if it had been there as long as the weed-choked railway sidings beside the cement elevators. Two of the five factories in town had shut down. Prices had dropped almost out of sight. You could see a matinee at the Regent theatre for a dime, including news, comedy, serial and double feature. Giant Redskin peanuts were ten cents a pound at Dutton's Nut Shoppe on the main street. Ice cream cones, chocolate bars, soft drinks were all a nickel. A full course meal at the Mayfair Cafe cost 35¢. None of which mattered a hill of beans if you didn't have two nickels to rub together, and were six weeks behind with the milkman. Somehow, though, most ball fans managed to scrape up two bits each summer to watch the All Stars.

As a stadium, I suppose Riverside Park wasn't much. The covered stands, not horseshoe-shaped as in New York's Polo Grounds, but sharply angled as if snapped in the middle, extended to just beyond first and third. Never painted, the wood was weathered to a bleached grey; the bench seats were slivery despite all the fans who had squirmed and shifted over them; and the tarpaper-covered roof sagged in both directions like Monday morning clotheslines hung with winter underwear.

There were a few boards missing from the outfield fence, parts of which were covered with signs: LEE-SON'S HARDWARE, EST. 1884 . . . ASHBY'S CYCLE & SPORTS . . . SUNSHINE DAIRY; YOU CAN WHIP OUR CREAM BUT YOU CAN'T BEAT OUR MILK. In straightaway center field, maybe 380 feet from home plate, there was a round, white-rimmed hole about the size of a pie plate. Put a ball through there and you got a free ton of coal, courtesy SANITARY ICE AND FUEL. Nobody had ever hit that part of the fence on the fly, except Chappie's catcher, who did it three or four times over the years. What he'd have done with a ton of coal, I don't know.

When my dad and I got there that evening, game time was at least an hour and a half away. The shadows reached almost to second base by then, but the sun, slanting through the clouds that were beginning to break up, bathed the outfield with brilliant rays.

Chappie's All Stars had finished setting up the lights. A few of them were in the visiting team's dugout, the rest sprawled around on the grass in the shade in front of it. Seeing them again in their grey uniforms with the black caps and letters, I got that same feeling, almost of awe, certainly of respect. I recognized some of them from other years—the big-seated catcher who could hit the ball into the next county if he felt like it; the left-hander who was taller and skinnier than anybody I'd ever seen; the fidgety shortstop who pounced on ground balls the way a farm cat pins down a mouse.

And Chappie. Blacker than any of his players, as black as the ton of coal waiting for whoever hit a ball through that hole in center field, I spotted him right away. He seldom did anything to attract attention, and he was nothing special to look at, but your eyes just went to him—I don't know why. That evening he had one foot up on the green railing that ran along the left field line, and was leaning forward, elbows on one boney knee, as he talked to Knotty Lee, our manager.

A few minutes later the All Stars wandered out onto the field, two or three at first, then others, finally them all. Playing every day as they did, you'd think they would have been fed up with pre-game rituals, but I had the feeling that they were impatient to get back out there again, as if it was the one place where they really felt at home. They took turns throwing for batting practice. Loose, easy, lots of laughter. The big catcher blasted three or four into deep center field. Each time he got hold of one the shortstop would turn and follow its path with glee. "Can't find the hole, man" he'd cackle in a high-pitched voice. "Don't matter how long it is, if you can't stick it in

7

there." The catcher didn't appreciate it much.

When they were finished, our team went out for infield practice, fat old Knotty going to the plate to hit grounders. Russ Taylor, our first baseman, had had to put in a couple of extra hours at the tool and die works and hadn't shown up yet, although he'd be there for the game. Nobody turned down overtime in the summer of 1933. Knotty could have used one of his outfielders, but instead he looked over at me and motioned toward first base.

It was nothing special. I always took my first base mitt with me to the ball park, slung on my belt by its strap or folded in my hip pocket. Often I'd go out and shag flies or field throw-ins for the batting practice pitchers before a game. A few times I'd filled in at first. That had started when I was about twelve, I guess, and the players had come to accept it—probably because they liked my old man.

So I trotted out to cover the bag, maybe a little more nervous than usual because the All Stars were there. But I did all right, fielding everything that came my way except for a couple of wide throws that went by me to the grandstand. They would have been scored as throwing errors anyway.

It was just about over when I heard a voice, not loud but deep and kind of gravelly, behind me.

"You lookin' to be a first baseman?"

Surprised, I glanced around. It was Chappie Johnson. He was standing just back of the chalk-lined coach's box, his hands pushed down into his hip pockets.

"I guess so."

"Well, is you, or ain't you?"

8

He scared me, not through anything particular in his manner, but just because of who he was. Up close I could see kinky grey hair curling out from between his black face and his dusty black baseball cap. And deep, purple-edged creases, like he'd squinted into a million suns. And there was a scrunched-up look to his dark features—a look that was both faintly mischievous and slightly evil at the same time.

"All right," I said, "that's what I want."

He shook his head kind of sadly. "Ain't gonna make it, not that way."

"What do you mean?"

"It's yo' feet."

I stared at him; you don't catch the ball with your feet.

"Yo' feet," he repeated, glancing at the bag. "They glued to that thing?"

"I have to touch it, don't I?"

He laughed. "You don't gotta stomp it to death. You like a baby bird, 'fraid to leave the nest. Hafta make the play first, then feel for it with your toe . . . just kinda flick it, light like."

"You show me?" I should have been too scared to ask, but somehow I wasn't.

He reached out and took the first base mitt from my hand. "Throw me a few," he said.

The All Stars were putting on their famous pepper game by then, and all eyes were directed toward the third base side. It was some act, the ball going back and forth, erratically, crazily, like the metal sphere in a pinball machine, only with rhythm.

Chappie and I had the first base area all to ourselves. I went back about 30 feet and began to throw to him. I threw wide right, wide left, into the dirt, over his head. Each time he'd catch the ball in my well worn mitt, and then one foot would dart back like a snake's tongue and just brush some part of the bag. He wasn't young, and he didn't seem to move real quick; but he got throws I couldn't have reached, not and touch that sack. It was as if there was elastic in those old legs, or some kind of extension, so that he could stretch them out a foot or more when he had to.

"Now you try it," he said after a while. He started toward me, tossing the mitt in my direction as I flipped the ball to him. We met half-way.

"Gotta range around," he said. "Don't be like some damn plant, growin' roots."

"Okay."

"Make the play first—*then* reach out for it. You know what I'm sayin'?"

"I'll try."

Then he was throwing to me as I had thrown to him. High, wide, low. I caught most of them, but three or four got by me.

"Get out offa there," he hollered. "Show me some space 'tween you and it."

I wanted to do what he said, but I felt lost if I didn't have one foot on the bag. What good did it do catching the ball if I couldn't find the base to make the out?

"Don't catch it, you ain't got no play," he said, "'cept maybe at second or third after you gone and got it."

He kept throwing. I didn't miss any more after that, but often I couldn't find the bag after making a catch, though I probed around for it like a blind dentist trying to locate a small cavity. Between throws I kept glancing over my shoulder to see where it was.

Chappie shook his head again, took a few steps toward me.

"No, no" he said, "don't go doin' that. Ain't no good lookin'. You gotta *feel* where it's at."

He paused, trying to think of some way to explain what was so clear in his mind.

"You play the piano?"

"No," I told him.

"That's what it's like," he said. "Gotta touch them keys 'thout thinkin' 'bout it."

I had only the vaguest glimmer of what he was saying, but I did my best as he started to throw again. It was strange, being out there, just the two of us. I didn't have time to wonder why he was going to the trouble of helping me, a kid from a nothing town in Ontario.

And, as we continued, there were two or three times when my groping toe *did* somehow find that square of stuffed canvas after fielding a wide throw. Just a couple of times. But when it happened I felt a lot taller.

Then, too soon, it was over.

Chappie came walking over to me, tossing the ball from one hand to the other.

"They's about ready to start now," he said. "You learn anything?"

I nodded. "A little."

"Won't come in one day."

"No."

He turned away and started for home plate, taking a lineup card from his hip pocket as he went to meet the umpires. He kind of ambled, and I saw that his thin,

11

black-stockinged legs were bowed. The stands were almost full by then and out of the corner of my eye I saw my dad duck into the weather-beaten press box.

"Thanks, Chappie," I called after him.

He stopped, and slowly spun around.

"My players call me 'Mr. Johnson'," he said.

# *II*

*June, 1939.*

Ponderously, the freight train began to slow; you could feel the drag coming back in a chain reaction of jolts and shunts from the front end. A water stop. The tank of the big 6000 engine hadn't been filled since around noon and must be as thirsty as I was.

I went to the open door of the boxcar and stood there, legs braced, one hand holding tight to the frame; freight engineers liked to manhandle their trains, and a rough shot of the brakes could send you sprawling across the floor, burning the skin off your knees and hands, breaking your bones—or spit you out, twisting grotesquely in the air, onto the dropping-away cinder banks of the road bed.

Bits of grime, sucked up by the sausage-linked mass of iron, steel and wood, stung my cheeks and got into my eyes. The acrid smell of coal smoke burned at the back of my nose, and filled my lungs. The flanged wheels, always ready to take off someone's legs, squealed and groaned and clickety-clacked monotonously over the rail joints beneath my feet. The draft tore at my hair.

Outside, the Canadian prairies rolled by as they had for two, maybe three days—from the Alberta foothills, clear across Saskatchewan, now somewhere in Manitoba. Who was counting, or cared where we were? It was all as flat and smooth as a sheet on an empty hospital bed, if not as clean. An infinite sameness, without features . . . without identifying scars or fingerprints. Almost, but not quite without people; now and again a wire fence, a clump of windbreak trees, a huddled cluster of farm buildings, a stretch of dirt road, a string of telephone poles, diminishing into matchsticks and fading finally into the heat haze on the horizon.

Talk was that the wheat looked good so far. Not that you could tell much just coming up to the end of June. Crops had been better the last couple of years, and people liked to think that the worst was over, that the freak time of drought and drifting top soil that blacked out the sun had best be forgotten. But who knew? A lot of things could happen before the heads filled out, the crops were taken off, and the grain flowed in golden streams. A lot of things. Hoppers. Blight. Rust. Scorching sun when you had to have rain. Grey skies and rotting dampness in the face of all your prayers for two or three clear, drying days to get the wheat in. Or an early, killing frost, after you'd watched it and nursed it and done everything a man could do. Then, all gone in one son of a bitch of a night, probably with a bright moon, when there was a skim of ice on the water pails in the morning.

To me, the land looked tired, beaten—or maybe it was

14

just the way I felt on that particular day. One thing for sure: I had to get off that damned freight, walk on solid ground for a while, get cleaned up, maybe find something to eat. I looked back into the car. My lone travelling companion, a good-natured, toothless man from down east, was still snoring in the corner, a couple of empty bottles of rubbing alcohol washing around him like flotsam near a ship wreck. He and I were members of a vanishing breed, the Golden Knights of the Road. Times were getting better, and you could find a job in most cities or towns if you wanted to look for one. The hobo jungles, where a wandering man could find somebody to talk to, brew a tin of tea, or heat his can of beans were gone, overgrown, as much a part of the past as the sod huts of the pioneers. Only a dwindling few were still riding the freights—out of habit, or perversity, or because there was no place they wanted to stay. Me, a Johnny-come-lately at it, for reasons that I neither understood nor thought much about. Not then anyway.

You still had to watch out for the railroad bulls, though. Maybe because they knew that their time too was about over, they were keener than ever to club you, walk on you with their hobnailed boots, get you thrown into some Godforsaken local pokey.

I waited at the door as the freight continued to grind down. Ahead I could see the town, a wart on the bare skin of the prairies. A few intersecting streets, a sprawl of low buildings, dominated by a quartet of taller, dark red, tombstone-like structures alongside the railway tracks. A four elevator town. We passed a white sign with black letters ALCONA YARDS, 1 MILE. So what? Alcona, Neepawa, Minnedosa,

Portage la Prairie—places where other people lived.

The trick was in the timing: jump too soon and you could wind up with a multiple fracture or two; delay too long and the railroad bulls would be all over you before you had a chance to run for it.

I waited until it seemed right, then crouched and pushed off, going with the forward motion as much as I could. I felt the shock in my heels, then catapulted on, my body twisting, my right shoulder plowing into the cinders. I managed to roll with the impact, and went tumbling down the grade into a weedfilled ditch. Good enough—a few scrapes, sore in a couple of places.

I got up, dusted myself off, and started toward the town, the small khaki dunnage bag slung over the shoulder that wasn't smarting. There wasn't much in it—a clean pair of shorts, a dirty pair of socks, an extra shirt, some odds and ends—and, down at the bottom where I could feel it bouncing against the small of my back, the first baseman's mitt.

Why had I carried that thing with me from town to town, province to province, season to season, coast to coast? I'd only had it out a couple of times that spring and summer—once to rub some Great Northern Railway piston grease into the pocket, another time to play catch with a fat section hand in Chicoutimi, Quebec. Why keep it with me? It was the only thing I had that mattered a damn.

I hopped a wire fence and walked across a field toward the nearest houses, the prairie grass undulating around me like waves on a lake. A naked sun burned down out of a cloudless, 180-degree sky. The wind was hot and airless, as if it had blown across a thousand miles of desert, and dried the sweat on my face as quickly as it formed.

Prairie towns don't merge with the land around them. There are no outskirts, there is no transition. They just go out as far as they have to and then quit. Where a street ends, there the wheat begins.

I stepped up onto a crumbling cement sidewalk, and walked along it, grateful for the meager shade provided by a row of scraggly poplars. The street was deserted. The only person I saw was a woman with her hair in curlers, who stopped sweeping her verandah long enough to stare at me. I didn't read "Welcome to Alcona" in her eyes.

At the end of the second block there was a grade school, an old red brick building. The bell in the white tower was clanging loud enough to wake my late boxcar buddy. Just as I got there the scarred green doors at either end of the building burst open, and out came two streams, one of boys, the other of girls. Joyous, running, milling, jumping around, their shrill voices chorused:

> *No more pencils,*
> *No more books,*
> *No more teachers' dirty looks*

Of course. It would be July in a day or two, and the kids had been turned loose for summer vacation. I envied them their happiness and their innocence and whatever it was they had been released to do. Let the fish bite, the lemonade be cold and refreshing, the berry pies hot and juicy, the thunder and lightning scary.

A block further on I came to the main street. Downtown Alcona was like the main drags of half a hundred other prairie towns. Wide. Wider than Toronto's Yonge Street or Winnipeg's Portage Avenue. If they had anything in the wheat country, it was room. A few cars and half-tons parked diagonally against the curbs. False fronts on the one-story, wooden buildings. A couple of garages, a butcher shop, a general store, a lawyer's office, a furniture and funeral establishment, a bakeshop, a Chinese restaurant. The jukebox in the Nanking restaurant was playing Artie Shaw's "Softly as in a Morning Sunrise" behind the wooden screen door.

In the hot sun the main street was almost deserted, but I knew I was being watched. A stranger in town represented both a break in the monotony and an intrusion. Who do you suppose he is? What's he want here?

After the J. Greening General Store, there were more houses. It was getting on in the afternoon and I was hungry. There was a red brick house next to a church, probably the manse where the minister lived. I went up the walk between neatly kept flower beds, and onto a wide verandah. It was shaded, and I could smell lilacs.

I knocked, and a few seconds later a woman appeared out of the deeper shadows of the interior. Her grey hair was drawn back in a bun, and she was wearing a housedress and apron. Beyond her I could hear the muted sounds of a radio. A news announcer was assuring his listeners that there was little chance of war in Europe; Hitler was just running another bluff over Poland, and would probably get his way again.

"Good day, ma'am. I wonder if you could spare me a glass of water, maybe something to eat. I'd. . . ."

A heavy, inside door was slammed in my face and I

18

heard a bolt slide into place. Chalk up one for Christian charity. Well, what the hell; the summer before a Lethbridge woman had dumped a tub of laundry water over me, including a soapy pair of grey, woolen work socks. Good socks too—I wore them most of the time.

The next house or the one after that might have paid off, but I didn't have much heart for it. Bumming a meal was getting harder all the time. Funny about that: when they'd had hardly anything themselves, most would share it with you; but now that times were getting better, people were becoming more possessive, more protective of what they had. We're all-right, look out for yourself. It wasn't as though an able-bodied man couldn't find work, not if he wanted to look for it.

I sat in the town park in the shade of a big, old poplar, leaning against its trunk, and eating a couple of stale bananas I'd salvaged from behind a fruit and vegetable store in some other town the night before.

After a while I got up and wandered along the stream until I came upon Alcona's war memorial. It was a slab of pink granite, polished on one side, and topped by a limestone cross. A rusting cannon stood nearby, the vagrant straws of a bird's nest trailing from its mouth. I read the place names carved into the ageless rock: Amiens, Ypres, Hill 70, the Somme, Corcelette, Vimy Ridge. And, below the dedication ('To Those who Fell in the Great War; Lest We Forget'), all that remained in Alcona of the young men who had gone away and been killed. Binkley, A.J. . . . . Dankowski, Alex . . . Lipton, Abner and Lipton, Henry . . . down to Young, Robert K. Seventeen names from that little prairie town, seventeen beds never returned to. So long ago and so far away. What the hell had it really mattered, any of it, to them?

From somewhere nearby I heard youthful voices—high-pitched, shouting, arguing. I went up a slight grade, followed a path between the trees, and came out into an open, grassy area. There were two boys, maybe 13 or 14. One held a bat with a heavily taped handle and a scruffy, grass-stained baseball. A hundred feet or so away the other stood, crouched and waiting, with a small and much-used fielder's glove on his left hand.

The batter tossed the ball up and hit a dying grounder out across the flat but uneven turf. The fielder moved to his left, judged the hop accurately, and came up with the ball.

"Got it!" he shouted triumphantly. "Two out!"

"So what?" the other kid asked defiantly. "I still got runners on second and third."

"That's where they'll stay too."

"Oh, yeah?"

I watched them for a few minutes, then opened the dunnage bag, rooted around inside, and pulled out the first base mitt. It would be good to throw again, to feel the sting of the ball, to jump for a high one.

"Can anybody else get into the game?"

Their heads jerked around simultaneously, surprised that they had an onlooker.

"Here," I shouted, pounding my left fist into the pocket of the mitt.

Reacting instinctively, the kid with the glove tossed the ball over. I threw it back, not hard but with a little something on it. Nobody had shown him how to cushion the impact by easing his glove back, and it must have stung. He didn't show it though.

"Well, what about it?" I asked.

"Can't," the kid with the bat said. "It's somethin' we made up—just for him and me."

"How's it work?"

"The tree's a single, past the rock there is two bases . . . like that. 'Less he catches it, then it's an out."

I looked at the fielder. "What do you say, kid?"

He shrugged. "It's his ball."

"Fair enough. You got a team in this town?"

"Supposed to have. Ain't much, though, this year."

"Not winning too many, eh?"

"Just one," he said. "Guess that ain't too many."

"Guess not."

"Wait 'till tonight, though," the kid with the bat put in. "They're gonna really get murdered."

"Oh?"

"Sure—the niggers is back again. You ever see 'em play?"

"I don't know."

"You ain't seen them 'coons, you ain't seen nothin'. Me and him's gonna sneak in after a couple o' innings."

"There's a sign over there," the other boy said, "on that second telephone pole, where the street is."

"Maybe I'll take a look," I told them.

I went across a little bridge, and walked up to a weathered cedar pole, pockmarked with linemen's spurs. There was a cardboard placard tacked to it, part of it printed, the rest hand-lettered in ink:

TONIGHT—FLOODLIGHT BASEBALL—TONIGHT!
CHAPPIE JOHNSON & HIS FAMOUS COLORED
ALL STARS VS. the Alcona Wheat Kings.
ACTION ! LAUGHS ! THRILLS !
Alcona Fair Grounds. 8 P.M. Adults 35¢, Kids 10¢

21

# *III*

Chappie must have bought about a million of those posters I thought. Even the prices of admission were the same. Only this one said 'Alcona Fair Grounds' instead of 'Riverside Park'. And it was 1939 instead of 1933.

Six years.

My father had died in the early spring of 1935, about the time the first tulips were poking up on the south side of houses, and the last, dirt-encrusted snow drifts dwindling away behind.

I turned away from the telephone pole, and started walking along the gravel shoulder of the street. There were no sidewalks out that far. A few minutes later a middle-aged man came along on a bicycle, the cuffs of his coveralls folded under black pant-clips. He told me how to get to the Alcona Fair Grounds.

"Stay on this street—oh, maybe a quarter mile—then turn right on King Street. Ain't no way to miss it."

"Thanks."

My father's funeral was from the vine-covered,

limestone Anglican church on the hill, about a block from the *Examiner*. He never went there except once in a while to listen to the carols on Christmas Eve. I sat beside my mother in the black limousine that followed the hearse down the curving driveway, and at every main intersection on the way to the cemetery a policeman saluted. And when we got back home neighboring women served little sandwiches and cookies and tea.

For weeks after that people would stop me on the street, people I never remembered seeing before, and tell me what a fine man he had been, and how he'd never done an unkind thing in his life. "I met him on the corner just a couple of nights before he died," one woman said, "and he asked me what I was doing out that late. 'Taking the bus,' I told him. 'Well,' he said, 'don't forget to bring it back by morning'." And to her that had been funny.

I dropped out of high school soon after that, bummed around, shot some pool, picked up a few bucks here and there, slept in most mornings. A couple of summers later I made the local team, which would have pleased my old man, and the second season Knotty Lee arranged a five game try-out for me with Ogdensburg of the Class 'D' Canadian-American League—which was as far back as you could get and still be called a pro.

I went one for 19 down there, and after the fifth game the manager took me aside. He was a quiet, kind man, who drank a lot to help him forget where he was.

"I gotta tell you the truth, kid," he said.

"Sure."

"You play the bag pretty good—yeah, better than a lot I've seen."

"Thanks" I said.

"But, as to hittin', hell, my mother-in-law could get you with her curve ball—and it don't break a half inch from the kitchen to the front door."

There wasn't anything to say.

"Ain't nothin' to be ashamed of. Line me up a hundred amateurs, and I guarantee to show you 99 can't hit the good breakin' stuff."

I nodded.

"And, remember, what you're seein' down here ain't that good. This here's the first rung and the last one."

"I know," I told him.

"Go back home and be a hero," he said. "Get a decent job, maybe. Baseball ain't everything."

"I appreciate it," I told him. "I really do."

Because he was both right and honest; an automatic out in the Can-Am League was never going to see the inside of Yankee Stadium unless he bought a ticket.

So I went home and finished out the season, hitting over .300 and going four-for-four in the final game, but resenting my teammates in a curious way. Whatever their self doubts, they could keep their secret dreams alive because none of them *knew* that they couldn't hit real pitching—except me. It was a little bit like the discharged mental patient who is the only one able to prove that he isn't crazy.

By the fall of that year there didn't seem to be much point in sticking around Trentville any longer. My mother, caught up in her church work, had enough insurance money to get by on, particularly if she didn't have me to feed. My grandfather, who used to take me for walks on Sunday mornings when I was a boy, died a couple of months after my father. Never sick a day in his life, he used to drink a glass of Scotch whisky every night before supper—never more and never less—and he got up to take a leak one night in his seventy-eighth year and dropped dead on the bathroom floor.

And the girl I'd been going out with since the seventh grade had decided that an assistant bank manager was a better bet as a marriage partner than a first baseman who couldn't hit curve balls, except the odd one that hung.

So, in the spring of 1938, when everyone else was going back to work, I hit the freights—just drifting, not going anywhere, not looking for anything in particular. I think I sensed that there was a war coming and nothing would matter much until it was over; but that may just be something I made up a lot later to tie the loose ends together.

And now it was almost July, 1939.

The Alcona Fair Grounds sprawled over a few acres of dead-flat prairie at the edge of town. The sun was still high in the sky as I went through the main, and no doubt only, gate. The afternoon breeze had died, and it was hotter than a pine knot fire. There wasn't a shimmer among the leaves of the few stately old poplars.

There were five or six wooden buildings, tin-roofed and badly in need of a coat of whitewash. Horticultural. Home Cooking. 4-H. Farm Machinery. Livestock. These were clustered around a rutted, weed-invaded, half-mile

25

track, which was used three days out of every year for harness racing.

And, off in one corner, was the baseball diamond. The grass and dandelions of the infield were freshly mowed, and a half-hearted attempt had been made to rake the base paths, but the overall result was about as even as a farm kitchen haircut, and you'd have to be a good guesser on ground balls. It was easy to imagine that you could break an ankle by stepping into a well-concealed gopher hole in the outfield, which was about the way the Indians and buffalo had left it.

Compared with the ball park in Alcona, Trentville's Riverside Park was right up there with the Polo Grounds in New York or Nevin Field in Detroit.

I wandered back to the gate. There was still no sign of activity except that a thin-faced old man, with hair that was yellow for want of washing, had opened up the ticket office in a rickety booth that seemed likely to collapse under the next salvo of greenish-white bird shit. He wasn't having much luck in trying to fit a reel of orange tickets onto a Rube Goldberg-type spindle to one side of the grubby counter.

"Be with you in a minute," he said, "soon as I get this stupid thing together."

"Don't hurry on my account," I told him.

"Useless goddamn contraption. Worst of it is I built the son of a whore myself," he chuckled. "You seen them before, the niggers?"

"A couple of times."

"Ain't they something'?"

"I won't argue about that."

26

"Wouldn't win, if you did. Best show I ever seen, and I go back a ways."

He stooped down to study his problem from a different angle.

"Seems a shame, don't it?"

"What does?" I asked.

"Why, they could be in the big leagues right now, a lot of them. Now you tell me if that ain't so. Wasn't their choice to be born 'coons."

"Just the way it is, I guess," I said. "You ever met Chappie himself?"

"Mr. Johnson? Sure as hell. Always stops by to say hello, and I'll tell you something'—I ain't never run across a better hand at lookin' after a business, black, white or piss-colored."

"I guess that's right."

"Don't need to guess. Beats me how he keeps that flea-bit operation goin'. That bus—oughta be in a museum somewheres. But he'll be here, sure as that sun's gonna go down."

Just then there was a click as the reel of tickets suddenly snapped into place.

"Well, whatta you know," he said, straightening up. "Guess you want a ticket. You got first choice. Any seat in the house, she's yours."

"Sorry, pops—if you could get into the World Series for a dime, I'd still have to listen on the radio."

"Figured as much. On the road, ain't ya?"

"That's right."

"Well, what the hell—my eyes ain't too good, and my memory's a sight worse."

"Thanks, but maybe I'll just hang around for a while."

27

"Suit yourself." He tore off a ticket, ripped it in two, and tossed one half across the counter to me. "When you're ready, just go on by."

I put the stub in my pocket, went out through the gate, and sank down in the tall grass with my back against the fence. It was a little cooler in the shade, and I might have dozed off except that I got thinking about the houses I could see, and how the people would be eating supper in the kitchens and coming later on to watch the ball game. That white stucco place with the green porch—what were they having? Maybe pork chops with applesauce, scalloped potatoes, creamed corn. The house next door made me think of baked beans with chunks of bacon, probably fresh homemade bread. And there, behind the tall hedge, that was definitely roast beef territory, with mashed potatoes, gravy, Yorkshire pudding, maybe some young peas.

I worked my way along the street, seeing and smelling and tasting all that food. There wasn't a person out there who was eating an over-ripe banana. Apple pie, maybe, and chocolate cake, and. . . .

"Here they come!"

The ticket-seller had come out to the gate, no doubt wanting to be able to say that he was the first to spot their arrival. I looked in the direction he nodded. There were two trails of dust about a mile away, but growing gradually larger against the flat horizon. I leaned forward, plucked a stalk of grass and put the fibrous end between my teeth. After a couple of minutes the two vehicles began to take on shape and form, and then they were coming in along the straight dirt road.

The bus pulled up a few feet from me, the dust drift-

28

ing away behind it, while the truck waited for the ticket-taker to lift the barrier and let it go on into the park. The bus door swung open and the players filed out. Yawning, scratching, stretching, they straggled past me, not looking around. Alcona was just that day's town; there had been a hundred like it before, and there were more to come than bore thinking about.

They still had the big catcher who teed off on balls that were never seen again, the ton of coal man. He got off the bus carrying a canvas bag with a dozen or so bat handles sticking out of it.

"How come I allus wind up with this thing?" he complained to nobody in particular as he went past.

The player in front of him glanced back. " 'Cause you so big and strong, B.G." he said.

" 'Cause I shit," the catcher replied.

"Oh, we all does that" the other player said, his face expressing exaggerated innocence. "You don't, you got more trouble than just totin' that little old bag. You *constipated*, man."

"Don't go big mouthin' me."

"Uh-uh."

"You doin' it."

"Here, give me a corner o' that thing."

The last man off the bus was Chappie Johnson. He looked older than the six years should have done to him. The creases in his face were deeper, the sparse frame thinner yet, the shoulders more stooped. Yet he walked with the same quick, bouncy, bow-legged steps that I remembered. And his eyes were just as bright and restless as they darted this way and that, taking in the details of the ball park entrance, watching the truck as it eased through the gate, keeping tab on his players as they single-filed in front of him. Like an old and very wary sheep dog.

I stood up, spitting out the well-chewed stalk of prairie grass.

"Mr. Johnson."

"Yeah." He stopped, his eyes crinkled up and his lips pushed out a little as he studied my face.

"I met you once."

"Could be." He stuck his face up close to mine, and suddenly there was a flash recollection. "Sure, sure— some place in Ontario . . . where all them lakes are. Belleville, maybe—or Peterborough, 'round there."

"That's pretty close."

"Close don't count for nothin'."

"It was Trentville. Joe Giffen's my name."

"Yeah, yeah—wanted to play first base, I got it now." How many places, how many faces since that long ago summer of 1933?

"That's right."

"Your daddy wrote for the newspaper. Kinda took a fancy to that man."

"He died four, five years ago."

He shook his head sadly. "Sure sorry to hear that. Damn, yes. What's you doin' 'way out west."

"Drifting, you know how it is," I told him.

Chappie laughed. "Ain't nobody knows better. Things all right?"

"Not good, not bad. You?"

"Real nice, 'cept for this last spell."

"What went wrong?"

"Lawd, most everything. My first sacker got took at

30

the border. Some hold-up back in Macon, they says. Think he mighta told me 'bout that, wouldn't you?"

"Seems so," I said.

"Well, he never. Then my odd man bust his leg in Brandon. Weren't no play, but he slid anyway. Took him into the hospital though, thank God for that."

"So you're down to what—ten players?"

He shook his head. "Worse. 'Nother cozzied up to a schoolteacher back a piece. Can't no way put up with that—uh, uh. Had to give him his bus ticket home."

"What's wrong with a schoolteacher?"

"Nothin', 'less she's white."

"Oh."

"See? You got one kinda trouble, you most likely got all kinds. So, my lefty plays first tonight—or I do."

"You?" He had to be at least fifty.

"Gotta do it from memory, looks like," Chappie shrugged. "That southpaw of mine's most blind, hasta kind of listen the ball in to the plate. Lawd, I doubt he could *find* first base."

"Might get hit on the head out there," I said.

We both thought that was kind of funny.

"Wouldn't never see it comin'," Chappie said. "Tell me—you ever get to be a ballplayer?"

I shrugged. "More or less, I suppose. Had a couple of pretty fair seasons before I left home."

"Trentville? That ain't bad ball, back there. What's the 'less' part of it?"

"Good curve balls."

"Uh, huh." Chappie glanced over his shoulder at the Alcona Fair Grounds. "Ain't likely to see a whole lot o' them in here."

31

"I wouldn't suppose so."

He looked back at me, and there was something new, something that had suddenly appealed to him, in his dark eyes.

"Well, how about it?" he asked.

"How about what?"

"You gonna play first base for me?"

# IV

I stared at him, waiting to be told that he was kidding.

"Me?" I asked after several seconds.

He shrugged. "Why not? Least you got good eyes."

Sure—blue ones.

"But, Chappie . . . your team . . . they're colored."

"I knows that. Ain't everybody? Don't never recall a face you could see through."

"Yeah, but my color is white."

"Don't have to be. You wouldn't be the first to pass."

Pass?

"How am I gonna do that?"

"Lampblack if we got any, shoe polish if we ain't. There's three or four bucks in it, 'pending on the gate."

I shook my head, unable to catch up with the screwball thing he was proposing. Joe Giffen—with the Colored All Stars?

He put his hand on my shoulder. "You gotta remember somethin'. All niggers look alike to them. Send the same guy up three times in a row, who's gonna know?

33

I hears that all the time. Won't nobody be lookin' close at you."

It was true. The All Stars I remembered were identified in my mind by their physical characteristics and abilities—the fat catcher, the string bean pitcher, the quick-as-a-cat shortstop; I couldn't see one individual black face—except, now, Chappie's.

Something else was bothering me, something still deeper than the color of my skin.

"Look, Chappie," I said, "maybe I could get away with being black, but I can't fake being good enough—not with your guys."

"Mr. Johnson," he said. "And, don't forget, I taught you all I knows 'bout playin' that bag. Comes to hittin', shit, we can score a hundred runs, should we need 'em."

The first base mitt in the duffle bag was resting against my ribs. I would never get another chance to play with a team as good as the All Stars. And I could surely use a few bucks.

"What the hell," I said.

He nodded, smiled. "Then let's get on with it. Just don't try nothin' fancy, that's all."

"Don't worry," I told him.

By eight o'clock the grandstand was full and fans were spilling out along the foul lines. Small town and farm people, the men mostly in work shirts, faded coveralls and straw hats; their wives wearing shapeless, mail-order housedresses. Families with kids in tow. Old men, alone. Babies, crying. Teen-age boys sporting windbreakers even on that hot evening: "Juvenile Hockey Champs, 1937–8." Giggling girls.

34

And there, in front of all 500 or so of them, was that sucker for the good breaking stuff, out of Trentville, Ontario—Joe Giffen.

In black face.

Crazy Joe Giffen.

A clown, without even having to do anything funny.

The uniform I was wearing had been made for two other guys, neither of them built anything like me. The shirt, with "Colored All Stars" across the front, was big enough for a family to camp out in; the pants would have been skin-tight on a praying mantis, and must have been tailored for some guy about eight feet tall. They figured to split like cedar kindling if I stretched far enough to scratch my knee. The borrowed spikes were so old they might have been worn by Home Run Baker; at least a size too small, the plates hurt like hell as they pushed up through the worn, thin-as-paper soles, making me walk like a stork with an advanced case of athlete's foot.

The only familiar thing was that old mitt of mine hanging loosely from my right hand.

Worst of all was the shoe polish. The smell of it was in my nose, the smart of it in my eyes, the taste of it in my mouth. At one and the same time it was greasy as bacon fat and stiff and taut as stretched parchment. I felt like I couldn't move anything except my lips and eyes. The beads of sweat ran down my face like drops of rain off a freshly waxed car.

Chappie had put the stuff on me in the back of the bus with the curtains pulled. Working quickly, his hands had darted between the flat, round tin of shoe polish and my face, ears, neck. He even rubbed some of it into my brown hair, the parts that would stick out from under a ball cap. I remember noticing that the color of the polish matched almost exactly the bluish black of his fingers.

"Lawd, Lawd," he'd said as he worked away, "lookin' more like it all the time. Be gettin' your mail in Memphis, Tennessee."

"Or in the Alcona jail."

"No, no, you gonna be just fine."

He did my arms and hands last, then stepped back to study the results.

"Not bad, if I says so myself."

"Can we get away with it? That's what I'm worried about."

"Booker T. Washington wouldn't of knowed the difference. Look for yo'self."

In the corner a shoelace held up a cracked, yellowing mirror. The face that looked back at me from it was grotesquely changed, terrifyingly unfamiliar. It didn't belong to Joe Giffen, son of a newspaper editor, but was that of some black ballplayer I'd never seen before. In its strangeness, it seemed to me an ugly face. A primitive, African face. The lips were thicker than mine and pinker, the cheek bones more prominent, the nostrils more flared, the eyes as bright as two half moons shining through the clouds of a night sky. The *blue* eyes.

"You satisfied?" Chappie had asked.

Satisfied? What I felt was an overpowering sense of panic, a frantic need to wipe away that veneer and become white—and clean—again. Where had Joe Giffen gone? What had become of me? It seemed all wrong that I could be turned into a nigger so quickly and easily; the difference should have been far greater than that.

But then, as the seconds passed, I began to get used to

it, to lose some of my fear of it. Hell, it was only shoe polish. I could be anonymous behind that mask—just another black face. And it would be fun to bring it off; to fool the good citizens of Alcona, Manitoba; to be able to say that once-upon-a-time I played with Chappie Johnson's Colored All Stars. You wouldn't meet somebody every day who could tell that to their grandchildren.

Then, too, if the image in the mirror was menacing and alien, it was also ridiculously incongruous. A joke. Shiny black face, neck, ears, chest, hands and arms— with the rest of me looking as pale and scrawny as a plucked stewing chicken. Somebody should have singed the hairs with a burning fold of newspaper; made me ready for Saturday morning market, or Sunday dinner on the farm—with plenty of gravy, new potatoes, carrots and onions, maybe dumplings.

I started to laugh.

Behind me, Chappie joined in, as if he'd been waiting for it. "You ready?" he asked.

"Sure . . . ready as I'll ever be."

"Better get out there, then. It's 'bout time for shadow ball."

I knew that routine from watching the All Stars back home. A kind of pantomime, the players pitched, caught, hit, fielded, threw, slid into bases, messed up plays, struck out, homered—all without using a ball.

"You want me in on that?" I'd asked him.

He had shrugged. "Nothin' to it. Shadow's the easiest ream there is."

"What's a ream?"

"Don't matter none now. Just act like it was a real

game. They'll cover for you."

And so I had left the bus, walked past the ancient ticket-taker, who hadn't even glanced my way, and gone around one end of the stand and out onto the infield, the spike plates cutting into the soles of my feet like pieces of sharp gravel.

I had thought I'd be nervous, but I wasn't; I was scared to death. The first two warm-up tosses got away from me, and the fans hooted. No wonder; Shirley Temple would have had both of them.

What was I doing out there? How had I let myself get talked into this? It was ridiculous to think that I could fool the fans for very long. And, anyway, black, white or polka dot, I just wasn't good enough to play with the All Stars.

My mind raced, looking for a way out. What if I let one more throw get by me, chased after it—and just kept on running the hell out of the ball park, out of the town, maybe clean out of the province?

Then I saw a black-and-white ballplayer, cap missing and brown hair flying in the wind, blue eyes gleaming wildly, in a uniform made for Laurel and Hardy, high stepping as if on a bed of hot colds, tearing through those endless fields of wheat . . . and it was funny again.

Anyway, shadow ball was starting. Too late. Nothing to do but make the best of it.

I glanced quickly around at my new teammates. The hulking catcher was behind the plate. On the mound for the All Stars—for *us!*—was a tall right-hander, so skinny that he jangled like a wired-together skeleton. And the left fielder only had one arm! He'd catch a fly, flip the ball in the air while he tucked the glove under his stump, catch it in his bare hand, and fire it in—all in one motion. Any runner who tried to take an extra base on him would be in for a big surprise.

At first the local players were self-conscious about taking part in the shadow ball, but they soon found out— as I did—that the All Stars would carry them. They had the fans laughing from start to finish. Me too, some of the time.

Once the string bean pitcher dropped the "ball" in the middle of his windmill wind-up. Going to retrieve it, he accidentally kicked it farther away, then couldn't find it. The third baseman came over to help look for it . . . the shortstop . . . the rest of the players . . . the umpires—all milling around, heads down, searching. Finally the one-armed outfielder got an idea, jumped up on the catcher's back, took off his cap —and there "it" was.

Another time, with a man on first, the batter hit a grounder that the third baseman, shortstop and pitcher all fielded and threw to second. Taking the throws one after another, the second baseman turned it into a rib-cracker of a juggling act. Then, suddenly, all three "balls" were on their way to first. I improvised as best I could, jamming each into a hip pocket before catching the next. Chappie claimed that we had made six outs on that play, completing the inning and depriving the home team of their next turn at bat. After careful consideration, the home plate umpire agreed.

I soon realized that the top clown on the All Stars was the shortstop, Sweetcorn Tatum. He had a high-pitched, squeaky voice that the fans seemed to love almost as much as he did. Like an enraged chipmunk,

Sweetcorn kept scolding and chattering away.

A hometown batter swung at a pitch, and Sweetcorn decided that he'd hit an infield pop-up on the left side. The shortstop maneuvered under it, waving everybody else off, including the charging center fielder.

"Ol' Sweetcorn got it," he hollered. "Oh, yeah, comin' down to Sweetcorn."

That pop-up must have been hit half-way to the moon. With all eyes centered on him, Sweetcorn moved to his right, then to his left, backed up, came forward, circled.

"Don't worry—I sees it all the way."

More shifting around under the world's highest rain-bringer.

"Won't be long now."

Then, at the last instant, he stepped aside, and hollered at the second baseman.

"You take it, Leon. Sweetcorn done got tired o' waitin'."

And the second sacker made a desperate lunge, catching the plummeting "ball" before sprawling into the dirt.

"You done good," Sweetcorn said, going over to help him up and ostentatiously dust him off, "only next time don't wait so long."

After a while I started to relax and enjoy it, even pretending that I had to make a sensational play by stretching high to catch a throw from deep short.

Sweetcorn didn't care much for that.

"Look at him!" he screamed, as he came charging across the infield. "He tryin' to make Ol' Sweetcorn look bad. It right in there, man—no call to go jivin' 'round like that!"

I ignored him because I didn't know what else to do and, after staring at me for a few seconds, Sweetcorn turned and walked back to his position.

A few minutes later the real game started, and it wasn't long before I began to see, close up, just how good Chappie's ballplayers really were. It was a lot different being out there with them.

The scarecrow right-hander's name was Luke Redding, and he had a fast ball that you really couldn't see. Once he only pretended to throw it, keeping the ball in his glove, but the batter swung just the same. And a couple of times B.G. Pickett, the catcher, put cherry bombs in his mitt when Luke really reared back and fired his high, hard one. Bang! He had a curve that took off like a bear going around a hornets' nest. He pitched one inning from second base, striking out the side on a dozen pitches. Batting against him, I would have gone about 0 for 743.

Often, of course, he eased up and let somebody hit the ball. In the second inning Malachi Brown, the third baseman, fielded a two-hopper and held the ball, waiting and waiting until the last possible second before throwing the runner out by half a step. It came across the infield like a rifle bullet, and I caught it partly in self-defense, and partly through luck. It hurt all the way up to my shoe-polished right ear.

Cotton Nash, at second, caught a towering pop-up in a giant-sized hip pocket.

Pete Simpson, the one-armed left fielder, threw a runner out at the plate by twenty feet, our big catcher grinning wickedly as he waited to apply the tag.

Woodrow Wilson Jones, who played in right, hit a

home run that must have rolled most of the way to Winnipeg.

Malachi Brown got the P.A. announcer to tell everybody he was going to bunt, then used a 12-inch bat to dribble the ball down the first base line like it had eyes. No infielder in baseball could have made a play on that bunt. Not satisfied, Malachi called time, returned to the batter's box, and did it all over again—this time using a bat that must have been six feet long.

After an inning or so I began to settle down and enjoy myself. Nobody in the stands seemed to be studying me, questioning whether I was really black or not. As for the funny stuff, the others played around me, asking nothing —but always making it appear that I was part of the routines.

The shoes felt better too after I borrowed Chappie's pocket knife and cut insoles out of a couple of discarded popcorn boxes. They still hurt, but I could run reasonably well and no longer figured to be a cripple for life by the end of the game.

Chappie had me batting eighth, and I went up for the first time in the second inning with two out and two on. "Now batting for the All Stars, the first baseman—Joe Giffen," the loudspeaker informed the fans. That startled me: didn't you have to change your name to be a nigger?

But then I was in the batter's box, looking out at the pitcher. From what I'd seen he didn't have much except red hair, a cap that looked like an army had marched over it, and about as much control as a drunk trying to piss into a bottle.

His first pitch was a slow curve that had triple written all over it, only it was about a foot over my head.

He got the next one right down the pipe—a fast ball, but not very. I hit it over the second baseman into right center for two bases, scoring both runners. It felt good to go in there standing up.

In the fifth I singled up the middle.

Two for two.

I was due to hit first in the seventh, by which time we had built up a 6–0 lead. Chappie called me over as we came off the field.

"Time to take three," he said.

"Strike out?"

"Yeah."

"Why?"

"No sense rubbin' it in. Only get somebody riled up."

"If you say so," I shrugged.

"Make it look good," he said, as I turned away.

I bunted foul, took a called second strike, then fanned on an outside fast ball. There were a few whistles and hand claps, but the Alcona fans didn't have much enthusiasm for their team, which they knew wasn't going to win if we played until the Second Coming.

It ended up something like 10–2.

"Don't do no harm lettin' them get a run or two," Chappie said. "They's nice young men, even if they can't play the game much."

After the final out the fans drifted away quickly, the local players among them, while the All Stars set about wrapping up the lighting system. I went out to help, but saw that I would only get in the way. Each man knew his job, and it came down like a circus big tent. Each piece had its proper place in the truck, ready for the next town.

When I got there Chappie was alone at the front of the

bus, entering figures in a black oilcloth notebook. He didn't look up, and I went to the back and began to strip off the sweaty uniform. As I bent to untie my shoes I heard the stitches begin to go in the back of the skin-tight pants. Well, they'd held out long enough.

"Yo' share come to three dollars and a quarter," Chappie said, half turning in his seat.

"That's fine. I can use it."

"I could make it twenty-five come the end of the week," he said.

It caught me completely by surprise.

"You let me stay?"

"Don't see no reason not." He smiled. "Could bring somebody in, but I'd have to pay his way. You come cheaper."

Just then the door opened and the players trooped in, their night's work finally done.

"I'm thinkin' of keepin' Mr. Giffen on a while," Chappie told them.

"Somebody to throw to, that's all I care about," Cotton Nash, the second baseman, said.

"He's half the right color now," B.G. Pickett, the catcher, put in. "Anyway, I farts white most of the time."

"You fart in all colors," Buck Yancey said.

"Glad you appreciates it," B.G. told him.

Chappie was satisfied. "Rules are simple," he said. "You pays for your own grub. You does your share with the lights. We'll show you that tomorrow. Don't argue with no umpires, less'n it's part of a ream. Stay outa trouble. And don't never go cuttin' a hog on me."

"Cuttin' a hog?"

44

"Don't miss the bus," Pete Simpson, the one-armed fielder, explained. "Gabriel, we call the old bastard. When she blows her horn, you better be there."

"Okay."

The others drifted away, Chappie returned to his accounts, and I went to the mirror in the back corner. I found a crumpled newspaper and started to rub away at the shoe polish. It didn't do much good: a few blurred smears came off, but I wasn't getting any lighter.

"Mr. Johnson?"

"Uh-huh."

"How am I supposed to get this stuff off?"

He turned his head slowly, and looked back at me.

"I wish I knew, son," he said. "I surely wish I knew."

# V

Rattling, swaying, bouncing, creaking, squeaking and groaning, Gabriel crawled over the flat, moonlit prairie; I don't think it could have made fifty if we'd had to make a run for it from a Sioux war party.

Sitting near the back and looking out the window, I wondered how Chappie managed to keep that old bucket-of-bolts on the road. Beneath my feet everything ground and grated against everything else. The frame, tortured and rusted, seemed ready to buckle at any moment. The rear axle had been bent and not straightened properly. The springs had said the hell with it several thousand miles back.

Outside, a three-quarter moon was washing the wheat fields with ghostly light. Now and again there was an orange pin-point from some farm house, well back from the road. I pictured men and women twisting the dials on their battery radios, trying to pick up WGN Chicago or WBEN Buffalo, New York.

It was all very lonesome, and a lot of things were going

through my mind. The world I somehow found myself part of was completely foreign to me, as alien as life on some other planet. A black planet. I tried, but couldn't foresee the adjustments I would have to make. It was all a big mistake. I didn't belong there. I should have gone back to the Alcona yards and waited for the next freight, east or west.

I had already learned a couple of things about the rules of the road, Colored All Stars' version. Just as every bird has its tree, every pike its stretch of weeds, ever timber wolf its range, each player had his own seat, made personal by pillows, pin-ups or whatever else expressed his tastes. I had inherited mine from the first baseman whose troubles with the law had finally caught up with him at the border. He, apparently, had been a leg man.

Sweetcorn Tatum was at the wheel of the bus, and Malachi Brown was alone in the cab of the truck behind us. On long hauls the drivers would be spelled off every hundred miles or so. Everybody took his turn except Chappie and Latimore Lee, the lefty, who could hardly see the bus, let alone drive it.

Among the other things gnawing at me was a terrible hunger. My stomach felt as empty as the Sahara Desert, and was grumbling away like a bad-tempered camel with indigestion. Didn't they ever stop to eat? If we just went on driving all night, I'd never live to see the morning.

Then, about twenty miles down the road from Alcona, Chappie put his notebook aside and peered out the window.

"Comin' up to it soon, Sweetcorn," he said. "On the right—blue and yella place, I seem to recall."

And there, around the next bend, it was. A big, raw,

barn-like building, its ugliness accentuated by a huge Neon sign—in blue and yellow: HAL'S FOOD STOP—OPEN 24 HOURS.

Chappie had known where to look for it, just as he knew every other place where a black man could get something to eat or a bed to sleep in, just as he knew the real redneck towns to pass on by, just as he remembered every level crossing, river, honest garage man, and maybe every last damn blade of grass, in North America.

As Sweetcorn eased the bus into the parking lot, Chappie came back down the aisle to my seat. Leaning over, he peeled a five dollar bill from the small roll he took from his pocket.

"This here's an advance," he said. "Be back in a half-hour."

"Sure—I'll tag along with the other guys."

He shook his head. "We'll be 'round back, in the kitchen."

"Well, all right, so will I then."

"Can't do that," he said. "The man serves whites, and he serves blacks, but he don't serve 'em together."

"You're saying I can't go with you?"

"Not me—him," Chappie said.

"The hell with it, then. I'll eat later."

"Up to you—just don't make no trouble," he said. " 'cause the next place that'll take us is forty miles on." Then he turned and followed his players off the bus and along the side of the building.

So I stayed behind, all alone, the garish blue and yellow glow from the sign ebbing and flowing beyond the window, and two opposing factions fighting to get the upper hand in my mind.

48

I was starved enough to chew the tape off a fungo bat, or make soup out of second base. There was hardly a trace of black left on my skin, not enough for anybody to notice, so all I had to do was walk over to that restaurant, maybe thirty feet away, go in, and order anything I pleased: a big steak with mushrooms—hell, *two* big steaks, if I felt like it.

Nothing could be simpler.

But I just wouldn't go in there. It wasn't because of any particular loyalty to my new teammates; everybody knew that niggers couldn't eat in restaurants—that's just the way things were. But since when couldn't a white guy go wherever the hell he wanted, including Hal's goddamn kitchen?

I concentrated my indignation and frustration on a truck driver at a window table inside the restaurant—a great hulk of a man, maybe forty, with a pimply, size eighteen neck, massive upper arms, fat hands, and a pregnant belly that swelled out like a spinnaker sail filled by a northwest blow. I watched him wolf down a big bowl of soup, three or four rolls, a hot beef sandwich with oceans of gravy and a sea of catsup, a mountain of home-fried potatoes and a hill of green peas, topped off with a slab of coconut cream pie that would have covered a third of home plate.

He was probably a decent enough guy who went to church on Sundays, remembered to phone his mother, and managed a Little League team in his home town, wherever that was; but, resenting my own stubbornness and the situation I found myself in, I also hated his mindless gluttony. I needed the food, he didn't.

Well, the hell with him and Hal and Chappie; the New

49

York Yankees would move to Moose Jaw, Saskatchewan, before I'd set foot in that restaurant.

I sat and brooded and felt all mixed up and wondered why I'd ever listened to Chappie, and gradually it began to seem more ridiculous than outrageous, and then funny—or maybe the light headedness was brought on by hunger. A rhyme formed in my head, and I found myself singing it to the tune of "Can't Help Lovin' that Man of Mine":

> Whites eat out front,
> And blacks in the kitchen;
> Everyone eats someplace,
> Except for Joe Giffen—
> How come he don't get to eat nowhere?

I just kind of hummed it at first, then got carried away, and was belting it out like Cab Calloway when I saw them coming back to the bus, and cut it off in midchorus.

As always, Chappie brought up the rear, shepherding his players the way a hen partridge fusses and frets over her hatch of chicks. They dropped into their seats as they came to them, but Malachi Brown walked the length of the bus to hand me a brown paper bag.

"Your turn at the trough," he said.

Inside the bag there were some sandwiches wrapped in wax paper, a cardboard dish of french fries, two doughnuts and a half-pint carton of chocolate milk.

"Thanks," I said. "What do I owe?"

"Nothin'. It's on the man until pay day. He'll nail you then—you can count on it."

"Well, it's appreciated. I could sure eat the rear end out of a skunk."

"That's about what you got," he said, going back up the aisle.

By then Sweetcorn had us back on the highway, and was getting every mile he could out of a motor that was living on borrowed time. I ate everything except the paper bag, the wax paper and the milk carton. The fat truck driver would have been proud of me.

In the short time that took, all the lights were turned off, except Chappie's up front and Buck Yancey's in the seat across from me. The center fielder was reading, his back against the wall of the bus and his bare feet up on the seat. I'd caught the title of the book while I was eating: Stephen Crane's *The Red Badge of Courage*.

The air was stale and heavy. A few seats ahead B.G. Pickett was snoring with the monotonous regularity of a bull frog croaking on a hot night, and with a lot more volume.

It surprised me to see Yancey reading a book like that. I'd never thought about it much, but it didn't seem likely that niggers got a whole lot of education—maybe enough to add and subtract, like Chappie, and make out a few simple words. Some, I knew, couldn't even write their own names. What need would they have for anything more?

Becoming aware of my stare, Buck raised his eyes and looked across at me.

"Something on your mind, rookie?" he asked.

I was embarrassed. "No—can't get to sleep, that's all."

"Now that's ironic," he said, "because you are sur-rounded by some of the champion sleepers of all time."

I smiled. "They do all right, don't they?"

"Oh, yeah."

"Where we headed next?"

51

"Town called Brandon," he said. "Sixty, seventy miles, seems like. Don't recall it, myself."

"I do," I said. "Got run out of there once, a year or so back."

"Oh, yeah, what did you do?"

"Showed up uninvited," I said.

We shared a laugh over that, then I glanced at the book he had put down.

"What do you think of it?"

"This? You read it?"

"Yes."

"Then you don't have to ask."

"My father used to say it's the best book ever written about war," I said.

He thought about that. "Maybe—or *All Quiet on the Western Front.*"

"I don't know it," I told him.

"By a German guy—Remarque, his name is."

"Oh." I expected these guys to play ball better than me, but not to have read more. "You think there's going to be another one?"

"Always has been," he said, reaching up at the same time to turn out his light.

I switched off mine too, and the bus was in darkness except for a faint glow from the headlights, which silhouetted Sweetcorn at the wheel up front.

About a minute passed, and then Buck said: "Far as what's been bothering you: in school—the same as you, more or less."

"I . . ."

"The real question is: who teaches you to *want* to read, to learn?"

I thought about my father. "Yes, there has to be someone."

"We'll talk about it another time," he said.

I tried to fit my body into the too narrow, too right-angled seat, squirming and twisting to find some position that would be at least tolerably uncomfortable. About an hour later, just as I was finally about to doze off, the bus turned off the highway, bumped across a hundred yards or so of uneven ground, and came to a stop in the middle of God knew where.

Chappie's light came on, followed by others, one after another.

"All right, we is gone as far as we is gonna go," Sweet-corn Tatum hollered from the front. He had turned around in the driver's seat, and seemed to be enjoying his role. "Everybody out! This here's the last stop."

There were groans and mutterings of protest, but the players shuffled and straggled toward the front door. I was the last one off, apart from Chappie, and I stepped down into short grass that sparkled with dew. The moon was still high in the sky, and I saw that I was standing in a cleared area that looked like pasture land. The ghostly shapes of trees, mostly poplars and pines. A whippoorwill calling mournfully from some distance off. A few mosquitos. The sound of a river or stream nearby.

There was a figure just ahead of me.

"What's going on?" I asked.

It turned out to be Pete Simpson, the one-armed out-fielder.

"This here? You lookin' at our home 'way from home for this night."

"Where are we going to bunk?"

"Right where we is. Beats that shit house of a bus, don't it?"

"I guess so."

He moved away. Most of the other players made the transition without really waking up. Acting automatically, the way a sailor instinctively reaches for his life jacket when the alarm sounds, each had grabbed ground sheets, sleeping bags, blankets—whatever gear he had accumulated with which to make a bed. Within a few minutes the bodies of my teammates lay strewn around me like casualties from some battle. B.G. was snoring again.

That left Joe Giffen, who was sometimes white and sometimes black, and—it was beginning to seem—almost always confused. What to do? I'd slept in a lot of places over the past couple of years, but I couldn't see curling up in that wet grass; what I could see was waking up in the morning with pneumonia.

"Go on back inside, see what you can rustle up," a voice said. It was Chappie. "Take whatever you can find. Won't nobody mind, long as you give it back in the mornin'."

"Thanks."

I ransacked the bus and put together a pile of odds and ends like a soldier in Napoleon's army might have gathered during the retreat from Moscow—a couple of windbreakers, the emptied-out bat bag that B.G. always carried, a small square of oil-stained canvas, somebody's worn overcoat—even some towels from which to make a pillow.

Back out in the meadow, I found a depression in the

ground and fashioned a kind of squirrel's nest around me, spreading some things underneath, and pulling other things over me, shifting and tugging until it all came together. In the end I felt dry and comfortable and curiously secure, and I looked up at the stars that were twinkling beyond the radius of the moon's greater light.

Well, there I was with Chappie Johnson's Colored All Stars. And I hadn't done too badly in my first game; the recollection of those base hits still tingled in my wrists. Oh, sure, Fibber McGee could have gone two-for-four against that redheaded country boy—but I'd stung the ball pretty good, if I did say so myself.

The moon went behind the drifting clouds of my mind, and I was asleep. . . .

"Holy shit!"

It was Malachi Brown's voice, and it was the first thing I heard the next morning.

The first thing I *saw* was B.G. Pickett.

The mountain-that-squatted-like-a-catcher was as naked as a bull frog.

He was riding, more or less, the biggest horse that ever made manure.

And they were coming, the two of them, like a runaway fire engine, straight toward the camp.

The horse's eyes were wide, wild, full of blood; E.G.'s eyes were wide, too—and scared.

"Clear the track! Clear the track!" he was shouting. His great belly bounced and jiggled like a mound of chocolate pudding, as he hung on for dear life. Sweat was flying off him the way spray is torn from the crests of waves in a storm.

It was probably about seven o'clock in the morning.

The sun, already high in the sky, was probing through the trees, making the dew glisten on the grass. Around me, other players were throwing off the blanket of sleep, sitting up, rubbing their eyes . . . seeing what I was seeing.

"Look out!"

"What the—!"

"Jee-zus!"

B.G. and the horse were almost on top of us, and coming to beat hell. He was screaming like a frightened child, and laughing like a maniac.

"How I steer it? How I steer it?" he kept yelling.

We were all scrambling, running, crawling on hands and knees. Sweetcorn Tatum went up a nearby pine tree as if it was a step-ladder.

I waited until the last second, trying to guess which way the horse would go, then dove frantically to one side. Chunks of grass and dirt showered over me as I lay there, trying to cover my head with my arms.

Then the hoof beats were receding, and I sat up. The horse had gone right through the camp without stomping anybody, and it was charging on like Man o' War coming down the stretch at Churchill Downs.

"You stop it, now! You stop it!" B.G. was hollering.

The horse, of course, paid no attention. It looked, as Woodrow Wilson Jones said later, "like it might just keep on runnin', cleah to the No'th Pole." Then, when it saw the river, the horse threw on the brakes. He couldn't have stopped any more suddenly if he'd run into a mountain or if he'd turned instantly into stone. About a ton of turf, sand and gravel, spewed up by his dug-in hoofs, went flying out over the river.

So did B.G. He was launched like a hanging curve ball, and sailed on like a towering four-bagger with the wind behind it. The splash when he landed, maybe thirty feet from shore, would have swamped a canoe.

I laughed until my guts hurt. Some of the others threw themselves on the ground, kicking their feet, stomachs heaving, unable to control their hilarity.

Eventually the laughter was choked off by the realization that B.G. hadn't come up.

"You suppose that big fart cain't swim?" somebody asked.

"Hope not," Cotton Nash said. "Maybe he learn somethin' outa drowning."

"Don't have enough sense to pour piss out of a boot," Malachi Brown added.

Chappie was standing a few feet away from me.

"See to him," he said.

So some of us went down to the river and waded in. We could see bubbles coming up, and Buck Yancey and I reached down, got hold of B.G., and hauled him out. It wasn't easy, waterlogged as he was, but we managed to throw him up on the bank, where he lay, sputtering and gasping, like a fat old catfish.

"Shee-it, it wasn't more than four feet deep out there," Malachi Brown said.

"Woulda been all right, had he managed to get his belly under him," Sweetcorn Tatum agreed.

"Coulda laid a eel at the same time," Luke Redding put in.

After a minute or so B.G. began to come around. He spewed out a gallon or two of water, shook his head like a dog worrying a bone, and finally sat up. Then, realizing that he was going to live, he started laughing all over again.

" 'Meat'," Buck said to him, "just tell me one thing—what in the world were you doin' up on that horse?"

"Tryin' to kill us, that's what he was doin'," Sweetcorn said.

"Took a notion," B.G. said. "Never done it before."

"Hell, you ain't done it yet," Sweetcorn said.

"What you talkin' 'bout? I rode him, didn't I?"

"Sure, you did," Pete Simpson said, " 'bout like a flea rides a hound dog, chasin' a coon."

"You *controlled* him, man, all the way," Malachi said.

"I did, didn't I?"

"Right up 'til you come to the river," Malachi added.

"Watch your mouth," B.G. said, struggling to his feet.

A few minutes later Buck and Woodrow had a good fire going, and were frying eggs, making toast, and brewing coffee in a couple of lard pails. The eggs had been provided by Latimore Lee. The southpaw pitcher, who could hardly see his hand in front of his face, had a kind of sixth sense when it came to eggs; I think he could have found a hen house on the moon. How he did it, and how he managed to evade the often quick-triggered farmers and their yappy dogs, were his trade secrets. Nobody asked questions; he'd just slip away before dawn and come back with the eggs—that was good enough for the All Stars.

"What's keepin' the 'Eggman'?" somebody might complain if breakfast was a little late.

"He sure draggin' this mo'nin'."

But he always showed up with his beat-up wicker basket filled to the brim. There were a few old teeth marks on his skinny ass, but, as far as anybody knew, he'd never been caught.

"It's ready," Chappie called out, and I took my place in the chow line. Plates, mugs, knives and forks, along with salt, pepper, milk and sugar, were on a card table with rickety legs that had been set up near the fire. It was an established rule that Sweetcorn Tatum was always first in line. Pete Simpson, who was the cook that morning, gave everybody four eggs, sunnyside up—each player's share of the Eggman's score for the day; any extras went to B.G. You helped yourself to toast and coffee.

I went over and sat down with my back against the trunk of a poplar tree. The food was good, and it was nice there, with the sun high in the morning and the little river sparkling away. All kinds of birds were singing, and a big hawk kept circling in the blue sky, its shadow passing over me now and then. The episode with the horse behind us, there was a kind of gentleness in that mecca of rolling pasture land with the fringe of woods around it, and it was easy to forget the harsh emptiness that lay just beyond the trees.

"Joe?"

"Over here, Mr. Johnson."

"You'll be washin' up, you and Cotton."

"Sure."

On the All Stars everybody shared and everybody took turns. Each day had its chores; according to the rotation, you cooked, drove, did the dishes, swept out the bus, checked over the lights for dead bulbs and worn spots in the wiring. There was no written list of duties; you just learned how it worked, and did what you were supposed to do when it came around to you.

Cotton and I gathered up the dishes and the pans and other stuff, and took it all down to the river bank.

"I'll wash, 'n you do the dryin'," Cotton said. "Next time we'll switch."

"Sure," I told him, "that's fine with me."

"Ain't no other way," he said.

And that ended the conversation. Cotton was often a moody man, and when he chose to be silent, you couldn't have gotten two words out of him with a thumbscrew; might as well torture a turtle to make it talk. Other times he would laugh, joke, enjoy long discussions on a lot of different subjects. It would be a while before I came to understand a little of it, but even that first morning I sensed that he carried some deep scars, and was capable of great anger, hatred, bitterness, violence.

Possibly a good friend; certainly a dangerous enemy.

He scoured away the egg stains with soap flakes and handfuls of sand from the bed of the river, going about it with a practiced efficiency which I tried, with only partial success, to match on my end.

The next few hours were free time. Once in a while a car went by on the road, trailing dust, but mainly it was our own little world. Some of the players mended socks and sewed on buttons, things like that. One or two wrote letters. Some slept. Some did laundry. Malachi scrubbed his uniform and hung it in the sun to dry. Buck and Pete and I had a swim in the river. Latimore Lee, the Eggman, was fishing with a bamboo pole and a bobber.

"Ain't caught nothin' in four years," Pete said.

"Won't, either," Buck said, " 'less there's a hen layin' down there on the bottom."

Chappie spent part of the time letting out the pants and taking in the shirt of my uniform. He sat in the shade and worked patiently away, opening the seams with a razor blade, holding the needle between his teeth when he wasn't using it, drawing each stitch tight. It amused me to watch him, partly because I kept trying to imagine my old man doing that.

Late in the afternoon Buck Yancey, that day's driver, boarded the bus and blew Gabriel's horn. We gathered up our scattered belongings and answered the call.

"Where's yo' horse?" Sweetcorn cackled to our catcher. "You ain't 'bout to leave him here after all you been through together?"

"Get fucked," B.G. told him.

"Ah will," Sweetcorn said; "ain't no cause to worry 'bout that."

Soon we were rolling down the gravel highway again, the truck tucked in under the tail of our dust. Luke Redding was driving it.

We went along for an hour or so. Same damn prairie. A freight train, pencil-thin and maybe a hundred and twenty cars long, inching across the horizon. Farm houses every now and then. Why did they build them so far in from the highway? Must be hell plowing their way out in winter.

It was hot in the bus despite the dry, dusty air coming in through the windows. Nobody talked much. Behind me Pete Simpson was huddled in his corner, playing a mouth organ softly and to himself. Up toward the front

61

Malachi Brown and three or four others had renewed their marathon poker game.

About five o'clock in the afternoon our gravel road died where it ran into a paved highway. Buck Yancey moved his foot from the accelerator to the brake pedal as we approached the red stop sign. The country school on one corner was closed for the summer, but a dozen or so boys were playing ball beside it. Farm kids, maybe ten to fifteen years old. The ball they were using was wrapped around with black electricians' tape.

Sweetcorn Tatum was watching them from his window. "Hey, hey, what d'ya say?" he hollered, his squeaky voice excited, gleeful. "We show them how the All Stars play!"

"Yeah, yeah!"

"Stop a while, and make 'em smile!"

"Pull her over, big Buck!"

Yancey glanced back.

"Give me the word, Mr. Johnson," he said.

Chappie took a gold watch from a pocket of his blue serge vest, flipped back the cover, and looked at it.

"We runnin' ahead," he said. "Fifteen minutes won't hurt us none. No more, though."

"She-it," Buck said, shaking his head. But he eased the bus onto the shoulder of the road, braked it to a stop, and threw open the front door. Immediately Sweetcorn, B.G. and Pete Simpson clambered out, laughing and shouting, doing exaggerated jive steps, and playing an on-the-run pepper game as they crossed the road and went through the gate into the school yard.

"Niggers," Buck said, looking after them—just the one word, and half under his breath.

62

"Ain't doin' no harm I can see," Chappie said. "You could go along one of these times."

"I could fly this thing to Paris too," Buck said. "When I play the fool, I get paid for it."

I sensed that it was not a new conflict. And much later I came to realize that the best of the All Stars—the honest-to-God, should-be major leaguers—had stayed on the bus. The three who had gone were the razzle-dazzlers, the dipsy-doodlers, the entertainers; not that they weren't good ballplayers, just that maybe they weren't great.

"They only gettin' in a little fun," Chappie said.

"Sure."

Sweetcorn, especially, was having himself a time. A natural clown, he responded to an audience, any audience, the way a cavalry horse reacts to a bugle call. B.G. strutted around and stuck his big belly out further than ever. Pete laughed and looked loose, proud of the amazing things he could do with that one arm. But Sweetcorn was the Pied Piper.

The farm kids stopped their game when they saw the three of them coming across the road, and just stood wherever they were or backed off a step or two. The batter let the tip of the bat trail in the dirt, and the pitcher kept turning the lopsided ball over and over in his bare hand. They didn't know what was going on, and their eyes were wide, wary, and a little scared. I doubt if any of them had ever seen a black man before; certainly not one who could roll a baseball up one arm, across his shoulders and down the other, then spin it on the tip of his finger.

But pretty soon they began to cluster around. Sweetcorn and the other two put on some of their best reams, and before long the kids' mouths were as wide open as their eyes. One of them laughed, and it was contagious and spread through the school yard.

"Hey, did you *see* that?!"

"Holy crackers!"

On the bus, I laughed a couple of times too. And I thought of the scenes that would take place that summer evening around farm kitchen tables within five miles of there.

"We was just playin' ball, see, down by the school, and all of a sudden these guys come along . . ."

"What guys?"

"These niggers . . ."

"Oh, Jimmy!"

"I'm tellin' you, he caught the ball right round behind his back. Never seen nothin' like it."

"Eat up your beet greens."

"But . . ."

"They're good for you."

Meanwhile, Buck waited impatiently. After about twenty minutes, he turned to glance back at Chappie.

"That enough?" he asked.

Chappie looked at his watch again. "Best be movin' on," he said.

So Buck blew Gabriel's horn . . . four, five times.

At first the three across the road paid no attention, so caught up were they in the unscheduled, school yard performance.

Buck leaned on the button again.

And then Sweetcorn, B.G. and Pete came prancing and dancing back across the gravel road, waving good-bye and still keeping the ball in the air at all times. The kids lined up along the fence, watching until they climbed back onto the bus.

I could hear them cheering as Buck turned onto the paved highway.

An hour or so later the grain elevators of Brandon, Manitoba, came looming up out of the heat haze on the flat horizon.

# *VI*

I remember the game in Brandon, a big enough wheat town that you didn't have to count the grain elevators. There was a good crowd on hand, despite the ominous black clouds that had rolled across the sky in the early evening, and Chappie made us hustle to get in the four and a half innings required to make it an official contest so we wouldn't have to give the fans their money back. But, although the heat lightning was almost continuous in the southwest, the rain held off and I went two-for-four again—a ground single past the third baseman (who was no Pie Traynor), and a double that rattled off the fence on one bounce.

After that second game with the All Stars I began to settle into their play-and-get-on-the-bus routine; days and nights, towns, games quickly became jumbled like bits of colored paper in a kaleidoscope, and only a few images stand out clearly.

There was a night when I booted two routine ground balls, and another when I made a good play to turn a potential extra base hit into a double play. But such things were just occasional commas, punctuating a paragraph that stretched out, line by line, and town by town. At the time it didn't occur to me that sooner or later there would have to be a period.

We played games in Winnipeg and Carman, Manitoba, and then swung south, following the valley of the Red River past French-Canadian towns named after saints and dominated by the domes and crosses of their Roman Catholic churches, until we came to Emerson, which is where you pass into North Dakota.

About an hour after the game there we were approaching the border between Canada and the United States. Up ahead I could see the lights and signs and the booths where the Immigration men put in their shifts. On Chappie's instructions, I was still wearing my make-up.

"Cool, now," he said.

But I was apprehensive as we pulled up to a stop; I wasn't an American citizen, I wasn't black, and the only papers I had were for rolling cigarettes.

"It ain't in that's hard," Luke Redding said, turning to look back at me, "it's out."

It was a little after midnight by then and, apart from a North Dakota farmer's half-ton truck in the next aisle, we were the only traffic.

Maybe a minute went by, although it seemed like an hour, and then a man stepped out of the booth and looked up at Chappie's open window. He was tight-faced and wiry, a little stoop-shouldered, and his uniform was unpressed, faded, frayed at the neck and cuffs, and stained in a couple of places.

He was eating the thick crust of a sandwich, and he

gave the impression that he had all the time in the world.

Cotton Nash at the wheel swung open the door, and the Immigration official put one foot up on the bottom step.

"Well, well," he said, "the nigger ball club is back again." He removed his foot, stepped back a little, and studied the sign on Gabriel's side. "Chappie Johnson's All Stars—well, well."

"Howya doin', Champ?" Chappie asked from his seat near the front.

"Oh, me, I'm doin' just fine," the man said, pulling himself up onto the step again, and looking the length of the bus. " 'Cept for havin' to get the roof reshingled on that place of mine. Cost me an arm and a leg, that did. Let's see—how many aliens you got on board tonight, Mr. Johnson?"

"Aliens? I got a couple don't always make the hit-and-run when I tell 'em, that's all."

"Say about five, maybe?"

Chappie glanced back at us. "Five? That'd be about right, I guess." He got up, reached across, and shook hands with the runt of a man. I caught a glimpse of a bill folded in Chappie's palm just before it disappeared.

"Always nice doin' business with you," Chappie said.

"Come again real soon, you hear?" the Immigration official said, moving away to raise the barrier that would let us cross the border.

"Don't beat them Dakota boys too bad," he called after us.

"Find snot in your soup," Cotton said, half to himself.

So we rolled on into the United States of America.

The thing that impressed me most that first week or

so was Chappie's ability to handle the hundred and one details involved in getting the show from here to there, from one scheduled date to the next, from Nowheresville to Nothingtown. There was a lot to it, a lot more than just playing ball. He knew every fly-specked diner, every greasy spoon restaurant, every truck stop along the way where his players could get something to eat. Wherever we were, he knew some garage operator to call who would get up in the middle of the night to grind a set of valves or rebuild a carburetor. He knew where he could get a good deal on light bulbs, bats and balls, whatever we needed. He knew where the cops would be laying for us, waiting to hand out a ticket for driving 25 in a 30-mile zone. There was a file in his head of the few flea bag hotels that would take colored people, and where the bathrooms were, and how many cockroaches they had, and if they'd let you listen to the radio in the lobby.

He spent a lot of time on the telephone, calling ahead to confirm dates and arrangements, making sure that his posters had been put up.

"Ain't no use goin' if nobody knows you're comin'," he said once.

But the problem that plagued him most was one even he couldn't do anything about—the threat of rain. A washed-out game meant that there would be no gate receipts to set against expenses, and the All Stars' shoe string was never long enough to stretch further than tomorrow, or maybe the day after that; if more than 72 hours went by without some umpire hollering "Play ball!," there wouldn't have been enough gas money to make the next town—and there was no place to send for more.

So why did he do it? What prompted him to put up with all the aggravations and harassments, worrying and hustling away his life, his joints getting stiffer and his stomach angrier, kidneys being shaken apart as Gabriel rolled endlessly on from town to town— and clearing less out of it all than he could have made digging graves or emptying garbage cans back in Louisville, Kentucky?

It would never have occurred to me to ask him, but I think I know what his answer would have been. "Don't know nothin' else," he would have said. Which would have been true enough, as far as it went. Only it wasn't really that simple, of course. It was Chappie's outfit, his own and nobody else's. He had put it together himself, and he made it work, and he took pride in his ability to handle all the complicated logistics. He was, in Sweetcorn's favorite phrase about himself, "doin' it." Chappie Johnson was a somebody, if only in those three- and four-elevator towns we played. And, for all the injustices it had done to him, he loved the game of baseball—its sights and its sounds, its skills, its excitement, its peculiar poetry, its laughs.

And so he went on, year after year, criss-crossing America from the sugar cane stands of the Dominican Republic in winter to the wheat fields of the Canadian prairies in summer. The year before the team had played every day except for Christmas and when they were rained out. It was always warm where the All Stars were, and wherever that might be was Chappie's home —as they were his life.

Sometimes, when the occasion called for it, he would bow and scrape, and be servile, and say "Yassuh, yassuh . . ." like a nigger overseer on some Louisiana cotton plantation back in the slave days. He could play that role, all right; like when he'd slipped the money to that border guard to ease the way into North Dakota with no questions asked.

Chappie couldn't have liked those times. I was embarrassed for him, and resented the embarrassment each time I saw him crawl. And it stuck in the craw of some like Buck Yancey and Cotton Nash.

But he knew that it was part of how you got from this day to the next, from this town to the one after—of what you had to do to survive. He knew more than any of us.

"You does what you hafta do," he said.

Other times he could be tough.

I remember a night when we pulled up beside a gas pump outside a grubby looking country store. The owner was a skinny, middle-aged man who chewed the soggy butt of a roll-your-own cigarette that had gone out. He filled the tank of the bus, then cranked the indicator on the pump back to zero as the truck moved up to take its turn. He squeezed every drop he could out of the nozzle, the last cupful or so overflowing and dripping over the bumper and onto the gravel, then came around to Chappie's open window.

"That'll be seven-forty," he said.

Chappie had already put a five and two one dollar bills on the seat beside him. He opened his black coin purse, fished out three pennies and handed them, along with the paper money, through the window.

"This don't come to seven-forty," the man said, looking up at Chappie, his eyes wary.

"Neither did the pump," Chappie told him.

71

The man shifted his weight from one foot to the other. "You sayin' I'm cheatin' on ya?" he asked.

"I'm sayin' you could be tryin'," Chappie said. "Three-forty-three for the bus, three-sixty for the truck —seven dollars and three cents is what I make it."

"Don't give me none of that," the man said. "You better pay up."

"I just did," Chappie told him.

"Looks like this is something for the po-leece."

"Could be, at that," Chappie said.

The man spun around, stalked off across the lot, and went into the store. I could see him inside through the window. He put the money in the cash register, then slammed the drawer shut. A woman, even thinner than he was and with her hair pulled back tight into a bun, came over to talk with him. Occasionally one or the other of them would glance out at us. There was a phone on the wall in one corner, but he never went near it.

"Why don't we just haul ass outa here?" B.G. asked.

"No," Chappie said, "we'll wait."

"You already paid all that was comin' to him," Pete Simpson said.

"Ain't nothin' the cops like better than havin' some-body to chase," Chappie said. "He'd call, soon as we left."

About five minutes went by, and then the man came back out. He crossed over to the bus with quick steps, and with his head down, as if it was raining cats and dogs.

"Shoulda knowed better than to serve niggers," he said when he got around by Chappie's window. "Nothin' but trouble every damn time. Now, you go on

—just get the hell offa my place."

"We surely will that," Chappie said. " 'Fore we go, though, mind if I make a suggestion?"

"What the hell do you mean?"

"Next time we come by, get the windshields, will you? Them bugs squish up 'gainst there somethin' fierce this time of year."

I thought the thin man outside was going to have apoplexy, which wouldn't exactly have thrown the whole country into mourning. His face got wild and red, and it was some seconds before he could get any words out. But we were pulling away by then and laughing, all of us.

There was another night a couple of weeks later. The promoter in that particular town was a tall, very distinguished looking man with wavy grey hair who smiled most of the time, shouted greetings to all the local citizens who came within range of his deep voice, and waved at the rest. I think he was determined to shake hands with every man, woman and child in North America. He was also the Mayor, owned the funeral parlor and the pool hall, sold real estate and insurance, and was president of the Kiwanis Club, Past Grand Something-or-other in the Shriners, and an elder in his church—all of which he managed to let everybody know.

What he didn't make public was that he was a crook.

When we came out through the main gate after the game in his town he and Chappie were standing together near the ticket office. The Mayor was at his most charming; I'm sure he liked to say that he included some "mighty decent colored folk" among his vast legion of friends—in the appropriate company, of course.

We clustered around a short distance away, waiting for Chappie; nobody was ever in a hurry to board Gabriel unless it was pouring rain.

"The years come and go, but it's always a joy to have you here," he said. His smile swung around to where we were standing. "You and your wonderful boys, of course."

"Thank you, Mr. Mayor," Chappie said. "You sure got a nice little town here."

"Thank *you*. We like to think so. Well, shall we get to business?" He took a thin sheaf of folded bills from his pocket and laughed as he began to flip through them with his thumb. "Pleasure, too, of course."

"Ain't nothin' unpleasurable about money," Chappie said, taking it.

"And that's the truth," the Mayor said. "Well, here you are, your half of the gate receipts—comes to one hundred and twenty-two dollars and fifty cents. Not bad, eh, for a night's work?"

Chappie nodded. "Pretty good," he said, " 'cept not for this night's work."

The Mayor looked taken aback, perplexed. "I don't— I don't understand," he said, still smiling, though perhaps a shade less enthusiastically.

"Ain't nothin' to worry 'bout, Mr. Mayor," Chappie told him, " 'cept that it don't come to quite enough."

"What? There must be some mistake."

"Oh, I'm sure that's what it is, all right," Chappie said, "just an honest mistake anybody could make—or maybe a mis-cal-cue-lation. What I knows for sure is that I'm missin' 'bout nineteen dollars and a half, as of now."

"Let's not argue about it," the Mayor said, reaching

out to put one hand on Chappie's shoulder. "Let me assure you, we kept a careful record—right down to the last penny."

"Tell me then," Chappie said, stepping back, so that the Mayor's hand fell away, "how many paid admissions was there?"

"Oh, you'd have to ask the ticket-seller, I mean if you want it exact."

"And whereabouts would he be?" Chappie asked.

"I guess he's gone home by now," the Mayor said.

"Uh-huh," Chappie said, "then let me tell you. We drew 'round seven hundred and eighty adults, and 'bout a hundred and ten kids."

"You couldn't possibly know that," the Mayor said, smiling uncertainly.

"I knows it," Chappie said, " 'cause I counted them."

"You what?"

"Oh, I counts 'em," Chappie told him.

The Mayor shook his head in disbelief. "Why in the world would you do a thing like that?" he asked.

It was Chappie's turn to grin. "Comes in handy now and again," he said.

"Free passes," the Mayor said, with desperate inspiration, "you forgot about them."

"I ain't tryin' to get re-elected," Chappie said. Then he glanced over at us. "Any of you invite some folks?"

"Ain't never even shook hands with nobody in this town," Sweetcorn said.

"This is ridiculous," the Mayor said. "I'm not going to stand around here arguing all night." He took a ten dollar bill from his pocket and held it out in front of him. "Here—how will this do?"

Chappie peered at the bill, which was folded length-wise.

"Do just fine," he said, "long as there's another one layin' there next to it."

"Oh, for Christ's sake," the Mayor said, going to his pocket one more time.

Chappie took the two tens.

"That 'bout covers it," he said.

His Honor, no longer smiling, disappeared through the main gate, his heels kicking up little clouds of dust, and we all headed for the bus.

"I never knew 'bout that," Latimore Lee said.

" 'Bout what?"

"Countin' the people."

"Oh, I doesn't," Chappie said, " 'cept when I knows I can't trust the man."

# *VII*

On the evening of July 6, 1939, about a week after I
joined the All Stars, Joe Louis defended his world heavyweight title against a lumbering hulk named Two-Ton
Tony Galento. The fight took place at Yankee Stadium
in New York City.

Over the year or so before that the Brown Bomber had
run up an impressive string of victories, mostly KO's,
over James J. Braddock, Max Schmeling, Tommy Farr,
Nathan Mann, Henry Thomas and a couple of others,
and many people were saying that he was the greatest
heavyweight boxer of all time. Galento, the current
white hope to dethrone the hard-punching Negro champion, was nicknamed "the Beer Barrel." According to
what I'd read in the newspapers, he was built like the
trunk of a Giant Redwood tree, had the strength of a bull
elephant, ignored pain, and had never heard of fear.
Two-Ton Tony only knew one way to fight, the sportswriters said, and that was to charge straight ahead, ab-
sorbing whatever punishment came his way, until he got

close enough to bludgeon his opponent to the canvas with a pile-driving, roundhouse right.

That night we wound up the ball game in record time, hustling through the reams, just making sure to win. Through previous visits to that town Chappie had come to know a man named Jim Stewart who ran a lunch counter and variety store on the main street. Jim was a quiet guy who loved sports, and he had invited us over to his place to listen to the fight on the radio.

On the way from the ball park after the game I became aware of an air of excitement among the other players. I hadn't felt anything like it before, nor would I again. There was anticipation in it and a festive spirit, and joy. It was as if we were going to a party. The bus was usually a quiet, weary place, but that one time it was filled with noisy chatter, shouts back and forth, laughter. They took part in it in different ways and to different degrees, according to their temperaments, but it was spontaneous, a shared thing, a unifying thing, a joyous thing.

I was glad that I understood some of it from being with them for that short while, though only a little, and that only dimly. It was that another black athlete, another black man, was standing that night at the very pinnacle of his profession. His skills, his talents, his brilliance were being spotlighted at the world's center stage; which, for a brief moment, lent some dignity to the harsh reality that theirs were being squandered, bled away, in the tank towns of America. If they weren't even allowed on the baseball ladder, the Brown Bomber had climbed to boxing's top rung. If they couldn't get into Yankee Stadium without buying a ticket, he could fill it.

We made it a little after ten-thirty. Jim's eatery was

closed, but we went along beside it and climbed some outside stairs to his flat on the second floor.

"Come on in," Jim greeted us, pushing open the screen door. "Just finished round one. Even, I'd say."

With all of us in there, the walls were bulging. The chesterfield and single chair went to the quickest, which didn't include Jim, who joined the rest of us on the floor. Luke and Malachi had brought some beer, for which we all chipped in, and they got busy, snapping off caps and passing bottles around.

But all of our attention was focused on the RCA Victor cabinet model radio that stood in one corner. From its cloth-covered speaker, laced with machine-carved walnut veneer, came the imagination-stirring sounds of the fight in faraway New York City. And the breathless, staccato commentary of veteran announcer Clem McCarthy, his voice perennially raspy from having described a hundred previous fights and a thousand horse races.

> *McCarthy:* . . . thus far in the fight. The champion's face showed no expression as he stalked his man. But Galento seemed scornful, contemptuous almost . . .
>
> *Sweetcorn:* He be it all right, 'fore he's through!
>
> *Woodrow:* When Joe get to him.
>
> *McCarthy:* And now there's the bell for round two . . .

We drank the beer as the second round went by, then the third. Around me, the room was charged with tension, excitement, suspense. Groans of frustration sup-

79

plied the verse for the chorus of cheers as Louis threw everything he had at the challenger—seemingly to no avail, for Galento kept waddling and stumbling forward on his pool table legs, taking the champion's best shots as if they were swats administered to a puppy with a rolled-up newspaper.

*McCarthy:* Louis scores with a left jab, a right, another right. Oh, there's a solid left hook by the champion, and a right uppercut. Another left. A right. All of those punches are landing, ladies and gentlemen, but the challenger doesn't seem to feel them. Galento is still wading in . . .

*Sweetcorn:* What the matter with that man?

*Malachi:* He made of stone!

*Woodrow:* Don't know enough to fall down.

*McCarthy:* . . . swarming all over him. Two more jabs by Louis. And another. I can't keep track of the punches. Now a wild right by Galento that grazes the chin of the champion. Not a damaging blow. Louis goes on the attack again. A left . . . and a hard right . . .

*Latimore:* Keep after him, champ! Keep after him.

*Chappie:* Hope he don't get arm weary.

*McCarthy:* I don't know how the challenger stays on his feet. And there's the end of round three.

Then it was the fourth, and Two-Ton Tony finally ran out of gas, or beer, or garlic, or whatever it was that had powered his brute strength and fired his great courage until then. Suddenly he wasn't a tree trunk any more, but only a log.

> *McCarthy:* Galento is staggering all over the ring. Louis with another right . . . and another. Wait a minute! It's all over! It's all over! Referee Artie Donovan is stopping the fight!

Bedlam in Yankee Stadium and at Jim Stewart's place.

> *Chorus:* Listen, listen . . .

The bell at ringside clanging repeatedly, insistently. Then the voice of Joe Audey, the ring announcer.

> *Audey:* Ladies and gentlemen, the winner by a technical knockout in the fourth round . . . and still the heavyweight champion of the world—Joe Louis!

We added our voices to those of the sixty-odd thousand in Yankee Stadium—cheering, whistling, slapping each other on the back. Joy. Happiness. Exultation.

I soon got the idea, though, that what the All Stars really felt was more an undercurrent of relief than a wave of rejoicing. And that both emotions were essentially very temporal, beginning to die even as they were born. Their hero, the Brown Bomber, had extended his lease on the penthouse of boxing that night; but there would be other challengers, and sooner or later there would be another tenant—whose skin might not be black. Joe Louis had won a battle that night, a holding action; but nobody had won a war.

81

Anyway, we sat around and kept working on the beer. We only had a short haul to make to the next town, and for once Chappie seemed relaxed and in no hurry to move on. It was nice to be in a home again, even in that seedy little place with its odds-and-ends of furniture and peeling wallpaper.

After a while Jim went downstairs to the kitchen of his place for a half-hour or so, after which he reappeared with stacks of freshly made ham and chicken sandwiches, dill pickles, butter tarts. Because of the ball game and the fight later he had hung the CLOSED sign in his window at supper time. Chappie and the others didn't seem to see anything ironic about being catered to by a man who wouldn't have sold them so much as a soda cracker at his lunch counter downstairs. That's just the way things were; and Jim couldn't change them any more than they could.

In the emotional afterglow of the fight, our host and I sat listening, he apparently as fascinated as I, as we were introduced to a world as foreign from our experience as Buckingham Palace or the White House.

The world of black sports.

Jesse Owens, for instance. At least I knew a little about him, and what he had done at the 1936 Olympics in Berlin. All those gold medals. A superb athlete who had made *Der Fuehrer* eat crow. Jim Crow.

But listening to Buck and Cotton and Malachi and the others that night, I realized how much more that three-year-old triumph had meant to the black people of America. Like the Brown Bomber, Jesse Owens was a symbol, an example, a flashing beacon in a sea of darkness. Proof that everybody didn't have to lose all the time. Not quite everybody, and not quite all the time.

Much the same with Henry Armstrong, who the sportswriters had dubbed "Hammerin' Henry." In 1937 he had won all 27 of his fights, and gained the featherweight title. The next year he had taken the welterweight crown from Barney Ross. In 1938 he had beaten Lou Ambers to become king of the lightweights. Monarch of three divisions at the same time! Unbelievable.

"Lucky for Louis he don't go one-ninety," B.G. said.

"Henry'd take him, I swear," Pete Simpson agreed.

"What good that do?" Cotton Nash asked. "Henry ain't no White Hope."

"He a skinny black hope," Sweetcorn said.

"Nigger 'gainst nigger."

"Oh, oh."

They talked about basketball too, and that was really foreign territory to me. I'd played a few times at the Y.M.C.A. in Trentville, but the scores of those games had been about 14–10 and 9–7. I just couldn't imagine that there were teams capable of running up 50 or 60 points, or that crowds of several thousand would turn out to see them play. But the All Stars knew all about it, the names of the teams and the names of the players, and who had averaged how many points a game the previous season.

"I'm tellin' you, the Globe Trotters is goin' to be the team to beat from now on," Sweetcorn said.

"The who?" Luke Redding asked.

"The *Harlem* Globe Trotters," Sweetcorn told him.

"Just who they got? Would you kindly tell me that? I mean, who they got?"

"You too dumb to know? Why they got Al Pullins and Sweet Willie Oliver . . . they got Inman Jackson. . . ."

"She-it, I mean what ballplayers they got?"

"You'll find out."

"Come on, man, the Rens eat them up."

"The who?"

"The *New York* Rens. Pappy Ricks and Fats Jenkins and Willie Smith just gonna run right over them guys from Harlem like shit through a goose."

But mostly, and naturally enough, they talked about baseball—black baseball. Jim Stewart and I came to know a little bit about Negro ball players and Negro ball clubs that we had never even heard of before. Players like Dave Malarcher, Judy Johnson, Buck Leonard, Nip Winters, John Henry Lloyd, Martin Dihigo; teams like the Bacharach Giants, Brooklyn Eagles, Indianapolis ABC's, Homestead Grays, Philadelphia Crawfords, New York Black Yankees, Cincinnati Clowns.

I didn't even know that there were Negro major leagues, let alone that the annual Black All Star Game had attracted almost 30,000 fans the previous summer.

"Where they playin' this year?" Pete Simpson asked.

"Comiskey Park, Chicago," Malachi said. "Near the end of August, I think it is. They say they gonna pack that place."

"They all be there," someone else said, "Josh and Cool Papa, all them big strutters."

"Ol' Satch, he be there."

"Oh, yeah!"

"Wait a minute," Jim Stewart said, "you're going too fast. Who's Satch?"

84

They looked at him with disbelief.

"You shittin' us, man?"

"No."

"Why, Leroy, that's who—Leroy Satchel Paige."

"He's pretty good?" Jim asked.

"Good! Hell, he struck out Rogers Hornsby five times in one game out there on the coast."

"Give Joe DiMaggio a banjo single, that's all, in how many games was it?"

"Five, I think, or six."

"No jive, man. He can do it all, ol' Satch."

They argued about the composition of an all-time all star Negro team, each vehemently defending his choices —an argument that would never be resolved.

"Who's the best you ever seen, Mr. Johnson?" Pete Simpson asked after a while.

"Well, now, that 'pends on the position," Chappie said. "Take shortstop, I gotta go with John Henry Lloyd. Hit .327 his last year—1930, I believe it was."

"Doesn't sound all that phenomenal," Jim Stewart said.

"Ain't that bad, though," Chappie said, "when you is forty-six years old."

"Oh."

Chappie thought things over for a while before going on.

"Comes to fieldin', now," he said, "I don't suppose we is gonna see nothin' slicker than Mr. Cool Papa Bell."

"No, no!"

"You got it right. He sure can go get 'em."

"What about catchin'?" B.G. asked.

"I hear the Elite Giants got a good one down there in Baltimore," Cotton Nash said.

"Who that be?"

"Name of Roy Campanella."

"Hell, he just a rookie," B.G. said.

"Ain't gonna stay one forever," Cotton told him. "Best to come up ever, some is sayin'."

"Could be," Chappie said, "but right now I gotta go along with Mr. Josh Gibson."

"Oh, yeah!"

"A cannon is what he is."

"I was there when he bust that one outa Yankee Stadium," Latimore Lee said.

"No, you wasn't," Buck Yancey said.

"What d'ya mean, man?"

"If everybody was there that day that says they was," Buck said, "they would have had eight million fans in that ball park."

"Well, shit—"

"Let me tell you 'bout somethin' I seen with my own eyes," Chappie said.

"Yeah, tell it."

"This was some years back, in Pittsburgh," Chappie began. "We was with the Homestead Grays then, me and Josh, and we was playin' the Philadelphia Crawfords."

We were all listening because he had done about everything there was to do in baseball, and because he was a good storyteller when something got him going.

"Come down to the ninth innin' that day, and we was losin' 4–3. Our first two guys got themselves out, me bein' one of them, but then Layton Hope got a single, and Josh come up to the plate."

He paused for a moment to sip his beer.

"The first pitch was a curve, which the ump called a strike. The next was a fast ball, and I don't know why their pitcher threw it. I guess he don't either. Anyway, it was a mistake. Come in around the letters, and Josh sure took a likin' to it."

Another swallow or two of beer.

"Now I seen some long 'taters in my time, don't think I ain't," he continued, "but nothin' that was took hold of like that."

He shook his head at the recollection.

"Lawd, God, it just climbin' and takin' off outa there 'till it went into the clouds. They was kinda low that day. Well, we all stood around, lookin' up, waitin' for that ball to come back down, only it never did."

"So what happened?" somebody asked.

"Ump got tired of waitin' after about fifteen minutes, and ruled it a home run. Wasn't nothin' else he could do."

"You won it 5–4," I said.

"Yes and no," Chappie said. "That ain't the end of it."

"How is that?"

"We come right back at it again the next day in Phillie," Chappie said. "Same teams, same umpires, all of us just moved over there."

He took an extra long pull at his beer.

"We was in the second inning," he said, "when a ball come down out of the sky."

"Oh, oh!"

"Their center fielder got under it. Everybody was screamin' and yellin'. Don't know why it didn't drive him right into the ground, but he hung onto it somehow. Musta come from a mile up, that ball."

We were all laughing.

"And then?" Jim Stewart managed to ask.

"Umpire looks over at Josh, who is sittin' on our bench" Chappie said, "and he hollers: 'You're out! You lose yestiday in Pittsburgh.' "

# VIII

We played some games in North Dakota—Grand Forks, Bismarck, Fargo—and then, about the middle of July, we came east into Minnesota. The big woods, and the hundreds of lakes made me think of Trentville, and I remembered that I hadn't written to my mother in months.

In most ways my life with the All Stars was working out pretty well. I was confident by then that I could hit the kind of pitching we were likely to see and playing the bag had never been much of a worry. I had invested eight bucks in a new pair of baseball shoes and no longer looked as if I was about to flap my wings and take off when I ran out onto the diamond.

The best thing, though, was the lampblack Chappie had found. It didn't smell or irritate my skin like the shoe polish, and a lot of the time I forgot that I was wearing it. I found myself leaving it on for longer and longer periods, first for a few hours, then from one game to the next. What was the point in taking it off? I don't think the others cared one way or the other, and I even began to feel more comfortable on the bus if I stayed black. I remember the first time I joined the poker game.

"You want in?" Malachi asked, looking back down the aisle.

And when it came time to eat I had only to put on my ball cap and go around to the kitchen with the others—remembering not to comb my hair or talk when there were whites around. The food we got was the same as they served out front, only cheaper.

Looking back, the prejudice we encountered at every hand is a puzzling thing. In those far northern states, and especially on the Canadian side of the border, people had had very little, if any, first-hand experience with blacks; yet the rules were as clearly established and as commonly accepted as if the two races had co-existed there for a thousand years. Don't stare at any white woman. Don't ask to be given a haircut. Don't contest for space on the sidewalks. Don't sit down on a stool and try to order a beer or a bowl of soup.

Know your place.

I don't suppose Jim Stewart really thought that his customers would desert him if he served us at his lunch counter, but why take the chance? We would be long gone by morning, but he would have to live with them —or without them—as the autumn leaves turned color and when the snows of winter drifted high outside his store windows.

It must all have been imported, I suppose—through the school books and the Bible, the magazine articles and the newspaper stories, the movies and the radio; but, however its seeds got there, and however alien it might have seemed among the Ukrainians and the Scandinavians and the other immigrants who had tamed that inhospitable land, the flat soil of the wheat and corn country had given it root, and it was very real. As real as frost in October.

We pulled into Hobblin, Minnesota, about five-thirty one afternoon. The first thing I remember about that town was that it was raining—not just a little thunderstorm that might clear up quickly, but a steady downpour that made the roadside ditches run like spring-swollen streams.

We went out to the ball park, but we knew right away that we wouldn't be playing there that night. Latimore Lee might have caught a few perch in the small lake around second base, but nobody was going to catch any baseballs for a day or two. Chappie and the local manager agreed to re-schedule the game for an open date we had three weeks later.

We welcomed the rare night off, especially Sweetcorn, who knew a girl there.

"Lover boy is back in town," he said, rubbing orange blossom brilliantine into his hair.

"That Ethel?" Malachi kidded him. "She is pure mullion, man."

"Jealousy ain't gonna get you no place," Sweetcorn told him.

"What's a mullion?" I asked Pete Simpson.

Malachi heard me. "A mullion is like a dog," he said, "only a million times uglier. Ain't nothin' badder than a mullion."

"A birthday cake, that's what she is," B.G. joined in.

"How you mean?" Sweetcorn asked.

"Everybody get a piece."

Sweetcorn threw a baseball shoe at him, one of the spikes taking a chip out of an arm rest.

"More like a railway track," Luke Redding said. "Gets laid all 'cross the country."

Some of the others wandered off to see if they could get into the local movie house. Another group went looking for something to eat.

I wanted two things—to be by myself for a while, and to find a place where I could take a long, hot shower. You get tired of being with the same people twenty-four hours a day, no matter who they are.

I put on the only clean shirt I had and walked to the main street, wearing my ball cap to cover up my hair. It had almost stopped raining by then, though it was still humid and very warm. I took my time, strolling along and looking in store windows. The few people I passed paid no particular attention to me.

After a couple of blocks I came to a red brick building with a turret on a corner. The local Y.M.C.A. I didn't know what they might think about a wandering black ballplayer, but it seemed worth a try. The man at the desk was reading a newspaper, and he didn't even look up as I walked across the marble floor of the high-ceilinged lobby. A couple of guys were shooting pool in an alcove to one side.

There was a glass door with a sign over it that said TO LOCKER ROOMS—MEMBERS ONLY. I opened it and went down some stairs. The place was as deserted as a Minnesota dugout in February. I stripped, helped myself to soap and towels from the unattended wicket, and was soon luxuriating under a jet of steaming hot water that

92

washed away sweat and dirt and doors and lampblack. I took my time, soaping myself all over three or four times. When I had finally had enough I stepped out, turned off the water, and dried my skin with the clean, rough towels that felt as if they'd been starched. Then I got dressed, stuffing the folded ball cap into my hip pocket as a final touch.

When I went back up to the lobby the man at the desk was still reading his newspaper. I wondered what he and the pool players would have made out of a stranger who went in black and came out white, but they had been too preoccupied with their own concerns to mark the phenomenon.

I went outside and filled my lungs with air. The rain was definitely over by then, and it was noticeably cooler. I felt clean and good and hungry and thirsty. Pools of water reflected the lights from the store windows. A red neon sign in the middle of the next block said BEER—BOWLING—FOOD, and I angled across the main street in that direction.

It was a big, barn-like place. There was a bar with a dozen or fifteen stools to one side, and a small dance floor, ringed with tables and chairs and dominated by a gaudy jukebox, on the other. Frank Sinatra and the Pied Pipers were singing "I'll Never Smile Again" when I went in. The clatter and rumble of tumbling pins came occasionally from the half-dozen ten pin lanes at the back.

I took one of the stools and ordered a beer. The man behind the bar was short and fat with thick, hairy arms. His other five or six customers were all older men, farmers by the way they were dressed.

"Looks like the rain's over at last," the bartender said, around the toothpick he was chewing.

"Sure did come down, though," I said.

"Too bad about the ball game gettin' washed out," he said. "We was supposed to have the niggers tonight."

"Oh?"

"Chappie Jackson and his All Stars, they call themselves. Come by every summer."

I started to say that his name was Johnson, but thought better of it.

"They put on a hell of a good show," the bartender said. "I never miss them myself, if I can get somebody to take care of this place for me."

"I'll have to watch for them," I told him. "Say, I'm kinda hungry . . ."

"You come to the right place," he said. "What'll it be? Steak, chicken, bacon 'n eggs, chili . . . you name it."

"The chili sounds good," I said.

"Best this side of Texas."

"Maybe with a stack of toast on the side—and another beer."

"Sure. Help yourself to a table. I'll bring it over when it's ready."

I took my beer with me and sat down at the edge of the dance floor. There were eighteen or twenty young people in that part of the establishment, a few jitterbugging to the music, the rest sitting at other tables. The jukebox was playing Herman's "Woodchoppers' Ball," the driving rhythm making the air pound.

I glanced around a couple of times, not wanting to intrude, and right away my eyes were drawn to a girl who was sitting with four or five friends at a table across the floor. She had long, blonde hair that curled and draped over her shoulders. She smiled a lot and laughed quietly from time to time. She was wearing a pale blue, short-sleeved sweater, a pleated skirt, white socks and saddle shoes. And she was so beautiful, and there was such a radiance about her, that I held my breath—the way you do when you come upon a deer in the woods and are afraid that the slightest movement will frighten it away.

After a few minutes the bartender brought my chili and toast, and it was as good as he had promised it would be—hot and spicy and satisfying. That and the cold beer. But all the time my mind was on the girl. She was the center of attention, and she was aware of it; but she accepted the homage gracefully, as an expected and familiar thing, to be lived with, and lived up to, and appreciated.

I couldn't restrain myself from looking in her direction. Twice our eyes met; hers were pools of pale blue, with darker ripples and a touch of fire, as you see sometimes in late October when a glint of sunlight penetrates the almost bare branches and makes jewels in the icy waters of a bubbling stream. Each time she broke off the contact quickly, and went back to talking and laughing with her friends. A couple of times she got up to dance, and I envied her partners for the seemingly casual way they draped an arm around her shoulders or spread a hand about her slender waist.

It was absurd, of course, because I wouldn't have had a chance with her even if I had been born in that town. The bartender brought me another beer, and I concentrated on it, no longer looking across the floor, resigned to the fact that I would soon have to start out on the long walk back to the bus.

First, though, a swan song. I went over to the jukebox, nickel in hand, and studied the typed labels. Goodman, Shaw, T.D., Eddie Howard with Dick Jergens' band, the Ink Spots.

"I was going to play some Ellington," a voice said.

I glanced back. Close up, the blue of her eyes was deeper, more intense.

"Why not?" I asked.

"I don't usually invite myself to other people's tables."

I shrugged. "Rules are made to be broken." Eloquent. She smiled. "Why did you stop looking at me?"

"Because I wanted to meet you—and there didn't seem to be any way."

"There was, though. What's your name?"

"Joe—Joe Giffen. Yours?"

"Mary Lou Everett. What are you doing in Hobblin, Joe Giffen?"

"Oh, just passing through."

"I bet you're a salesman."

"Kind of," I told her.

"Farm machinery?"

I shook my head.

"All right, I'll try again. How about paper and envelopes and things like that?"

"Not even close," I told her.

"You know I'll make you tell me in the long run, don't you?"

"I wouldn't be surprised," I said, and we both laughed.

"Right now I've got a good idea," I said.

"What's that?"

"Let's dance. Would you like to?"

"Uh-huh."

We went out onto the floor, which had been dusted with corn starch or talcum powder, and joined three or four other couples. The jukebox played Artie Shaw's version of "Deep Purple" and Jan Savitt's hard-riding "720 in the Books," and from the first moment I knew that the feel of her in my arms was something that would last for a long time. She was the best dancer I'd ever met.

After three or four numbers we went back to the table. I ordered some more beer and we shared a bowlful of potato chips, which I tasted for the first time that evening. But mostly we talked. It was as if both of us had been saving things up for a long time.

She told me about her life in Hobblin: how she had been a tomboy as a little girl, and then matured to become a cheerleader and the Homecoming Queen in high school. About her father, who had been a leading merchant and a hearty, generous man until he dropped dead of a heart attack two years ago that summer. About how life was pleasant and easy, but confining and restricting in that town of hers. And, more hesitantly, about how she thought she might like to go to New York and try to become a model.

I talked about Trentville, including some things I didn't even know were in my mind: how I used to walk down beside the river late each spring to look for the giant muskie that spawned in the shallow water by the railway bridge, and the hot meat pie my mother always had ready for me when I came home from a hockey game.

We danced again two or three times, and about ten-thirty some of her friends came over, two boys and another girl, and stood behind her.

"We're goin' down to Ziggy's for shakes," one of the boys said. He was tall, with light brown hair, and his broad shoulders bulked out the windbreaker he was wearing, the crest on the front of which said "HOBBLIN VIKINGS, Minnesota American Legion Baseball Champs, 1938."

"You coming, Mary Lou?" the girl asked.

"No, thanks," she said, shaking her head so her hair swirled around her shoulders. "You all run along. I'll see you tomorrow."

I liked that, as I liked the way she held my hand while the records were changing on the jukebox between dances, and the way she looked at me, and her smile.

The tall guy in the windbreaker didn't like it much, though.

"You're sure you know what you're doing?" he asked.

"When I'm not, I'll ask for your advice," she told him.

"Well, suit yourself."

"I intend to," Mary Lou said.

"Come on, Clyde," the other girl said. "We're wasting time."

"I guess we are at that," he said, glaring down at me. Then he followed the other two out past the bar to the front door.

After they had gone she was silent for a long moment, then smiled.

"That's just Clyde for you," she said. "He thinks he has to protect me."

"He could be right," I said.

"That's nice. I like that."

98

"So do I," I told her.

We stayed on for another hour, talking, sipping our beer, looking into each other's eyes, dancing now and again.

"I suppose I'd better be getting home," she said at last. "You'll walk me, won't you?"

"Nothing could stop me," I said, "but first, how about one last dance?"

"The home waltz?"

"Kind of," I said.

The place was almost deserted by then. We went over to the jukebox and stood side by side, holding hands. I pushed a coin into the slot and pressed the button for Duke Ellington's arrangement of "Where or When."

Then she was in my arms again, and her hair was a little damp at the temples from the more strenuous dancing we had done earlier, and there was a hint of perfume, and her cheek against mine, and our bodies close together.

The music came to an end, and I played the same song again. We moved slowly around the dance floor, our feet barely moving, and I didn't want it ever to end.

She pulled back her head for a moment, and looked up at me.

"Where?" she asked.

"In Hobblin, Minnesota," I said.

"And when?"

"Right now."

She moved her hand up and placed it lightly at the back of my neck.

"Let's get out of here," she said.

"Okay."

I paid the bartender and we went out and turned left along the main street.

"It isn't far," she said. "Nothing is in Hobblin."

About a block later I looked ahead and saw Buck Yancey, Luke Redding and Latimore Lee coming toward us on the same side of the street. I just managed to fight back the impulse to call out a greeting; it would have been so natural to stop and talk, to introduce them to Mary Lou. . . .

But they went on by without a hint of recognition, talking among themselves, not even glancing in our direction.

"They must belong to that nigger ball team," she said, looking back over her shoulder at them.

"I heard they were in town," I said.

"So are you," she said, "and that's much more important."

We turned off onto a side street. Big, leafy trees formed a canopy, the underside brushed by the street lights, overhead. The well cared for houses were set back behind hedges and lilac bushes. From one the voice of a radio news announcer drifted to us, reporting that the League of Nations was convening an emergency session in Geneva to discuss Europe's mounting international tensions. At another a circulating lawn sprinkler was throwing drops of water against the bushes, despite the drenching rain that had fallen all day.

"This is it," she said, after a couple of blocks, "the old homestead."

Her house was painted white, a comfortable looking, two-story place, much like its neighbors. We went along a flagstone walk between flower beds, and up onto the wide verandah. There was a light on over the front door, and another beyond the window of an upstairs bedroom.

She put a hand on my arm, and leaned close to whisper.

"Mother's still awake."

I nodded.

"Mary Lou, it's . . . I don't know . . . I'm just so glad I met you."

"Oh, Joe . . ."

We came into each other's arms, and I could feel her body moving under my hands, and we were kissing— tentatively at first, then with increasing passion and tenderness, mixed together in fluid and mysterious proportions.

"Mary Lou, is that you?" The voice came from upstairs.

She held a finger to her lips, and we waited in afraid-to-breathe silence. No use.

"I know you're down there," the voice said.

I felt a shiver run across Mary Lou's shoulders.

"Yes, Mother," she called out, resignedly, "I'm coming." Her face came back against mine. "I've got to go in," she whispered. "Will I ever see you again?"

"If you want to."

She drew her head back, and there was happiness in her eyes.

"Really?"

"I'll be back here in three weeks."

"So long!"

"It'll pass."

I held her close once more, and her lips were alive, a

101

image

girl's and a woman's, giving and demanding, and so much mine.

Then she was gone inside the house, the spring hasp closing the screen door behind her.

I stood there for a moment, and then I went down the path between the flower beds, along her street to the main drag, and then another seven or eight blocks to where the bus was parked outside the ball park. I was floating rather than walking, and there was music under the soles of my feet and all around me—"720 in the Books" . . . "Sunrise Serenade" . . . "Where or When." There was the sadness of parting, and the excitement that we would meet again. There was Mary Lou.

There was also hell to pay when I got back.

Almost everyone else had returned by then. A couple nodded as I went along the aisle, but nobody said anything. I thought the silent treatment might be a gag of some sort, and I was trying to figure out what they had cooked up for me as I slid into my seat. I was there about two minutes when Chappie turned around and looked back at me.

"Mr. Giffen, you 'spose I could talk to you?" he asked.

I went up and sat on the arm of the seat across from his, which was always reserved for his account books and the black tin box in which he kept the team funds.

"What's up?"

"I hear you met up with a gal tonight, a real good looker."

"That's right," I said, "I got lucky."

"You got poorer too. I gonna fine you ten bucks."

That was almost a half a week's pay.

"What for?" I asked. "I didn't cut a hog."

"I hear she was a white gal."

"Well, what the hell," I said, "I'm white."

"You is tonight, but you wasn't today, and you won't be tomorrow ... if you stay with this ball club, that is."

"Of course I want to stay, but—"

"Then you know the rules."

"Sure, Chappie—"

"Mr. Johnson."

"—I know the rules."

"You could get us into just as much trouble as anybody else," he said, "maybe more. So it's ten bucks, and you get to drive the truck tonight, even tho' it ain't your turn."

I looked at him for a long moment before I finally nodded.

"All right," I said.

"Got ourselves a long haul down to St. Cloud," he said. "Give you time to think it over."

So I wound up following the taillights of the bus through the black, empty night.

But what I thought about was Mary Lou Everett, and how I would find a way to see her again when we came back there in three weeks time.

# IX

"Tell him 'bout it," Sweetcorn said, "you know, 'bout what it was like."

"Oh, no," Malachi Brown said. "He don' wanta hear that stuff."

We were clustered around Sweetcorn's seat, four or five of us, as the bus swayed and rattled on toward the next stop. For once the poker game had been temporarily suspended, mainly because some of us were broke. A couple of days out of Hibbing, Chappie and the others seemed willing to forget about my brief encounter with Mary Lou, although she was never far from my mind.

"Sure," I told Malachi, "I'd like to hear."

"Ah, it was a long time back," Malachi said.

"How old was you?" Woodrow Wilson Jones asked.

" 'Bout fifteen, I think. But, shit, it weren't no big thing. I ain't the only one done time—B.G. and Latimore, they was in a while too."

"Not in the chain gang, they wasn't," Sweetcorn prompted.

104

"Ain't so different," Malachi said. But the point had been reached where he wanted to talk about it, and the words started to come out—not in a torrent, but like drops from a leaky tap.

He had been arrested for stealing biscuits from the glass-fronted case of a country store near Waycross, Georgia.

"I swear I never took nothin'," he said. "Shit, my daddy woulda killed me for takin' anything."

But the judge had arrived at a guilty verdict, and sentenced him to eighteen months hard labor.

"They used to take us out 'fore the sun was up in the mo'nin'," Malachi continued, "and we never was back 'till it come near dark. Cuttin' bush, we done mostly. Lawd, God, I never seen so many chiggers."

The low, swampy land had been infested with snakes, too; Malachi remembered chopping the heads off three big diamondbacks with his axe one forenoon.

"This time they had us diggin' gravel," he said, laughing at the recollection. "We'd wheelbarrow it 'cross this ridge, see, and dump it. Then 'nother gang'd fill them 'barrows 'n bring it right back again. I swear that gravel musta travelled a thousand miles 'fore we was done."

He had worked twelve to fourteen hours, six days a week. On Sundays the Warden would bring his family to listen to them sing spirituals.

"We was 'most too tired to stand up," he said, "but we done it. Oh, yeah, we got the beat goin' real good."

On workdays there was a twenty-minute break for lunch.

"Didn't never got to ask what was on the menu," Malachi went on. "Same thing every day—stew, they

105

said it was, with a few bits of potato and carrots. Supper-time, they might put a little meat in it—cat, most likely. Sure was a lot of them disappeared 'round there."

"Tell him 'bout takin' a crap," Sweetcorn said.

"Oh, Jesus" Malachi said, a smile spreading over his coal-black features. "Well, see, pissin' wasn't nothin'—you just done that wherever you was. But a shit—that was good for five, maybe ten minutes."

"Didn't pay to be constipated, though," Sweetcorn said, giggling.

"Oh, my, no" Malachi said, shaking his head. "You come back outa the bushes, you better have a stick with some on it!"

They all seemed to think that was as funny as hell.

As the days came and went, and the games, and the long nights, I learned more about the others. Some of it was just bits and pieces. I found out, for instance, that Latimore Lee came from a place called Willacoochee, Georgia, and Buck Redding from Gee's Bend, Arkansas.

The better I got to know Sweetcorn, the more I came to understand that he was a troubled, sometimes very mean, and potentially dangerous man. He might play pepper with country kids, act the carefree high strutter, and chatter away in that absurd bird-like voice of his, but there were dark and strange things brooding in the twisting caverns of his mind.

"My old man once told me never to trust a bear," Pete Simpson said once. "Sweetcorn, now, he's like that—be your best friend one minute, then come stompin' after you the next. I seen it happen."

Maybe the realization that he wasn't as good a ball-player as most of the others had something to do with it.

106

Not, mind you, that he was bad; Sweetcorn could make all of the plays at short, had an arm like a deer rifle, and would have hit around .300 in AA or maybe even AAA ball. Yet his talents, while substantial, fell short of big league standards.

Or, conversely, he might have felt a sense of superiority, even contempt, since he had reached his full potential as top clown with the All Stars, while the others, however much better they might be, had to accept roles beneath their full capabilities. Sweetcorn was a very good ballplayer with a natural ability to make people laugh; they were great ball players who had had to learn to be funny.

He was like a child in many ways, but he could be as unpredictable as a bouncing football and as vicious as a wolverine.

"I remember this time—in Boise, Idaho, I think it was," Buck Yancey told me. "Home town guy hit a pop-up 'bout a mile high. I could hear Sweetcorn yellin', but it was my ball all the way, so I took it."

He paused, shaking his head in disbelief.

"Apparently, though, he had figured out some kind of new ream, right then while the ball was in the air, and I spoiled it for him. How the hell was I supposed to know what was going on in his head?"

Another pause.

"Anyway, 'bout three days later I come back to the bus and everything I owned had been slashed to pieces—books I had, clothes, even the laces in my shoes. What a mess."

"Sweetcorn did that?" I asked.

"Sure, he did. Must have used a straight razor. And all

because I loused up a ream I didn't even know about. Didn't say a word at the time, but, see, he had it in his mind that he was gonna get me."

I spent more time with Buck than with any of the others, and only partly because we were neighbors on the bus. He was always trying to think things through, to learn, to understand, and he had a lot of ideas that were interesting to me, even when I didn't agree with them. We sat up most of one night talking about John Steinbeck's *The Grapes of Wrath*, which he had lent me to read. The book had come out a year or so before, I think.

"That man really sees things," Buck said. "It's not just us that gets shit on, it's all the poor people, white the same as black. Take those poor, dumb Okies—what did they have? No decent education, nobody to stand up for them in the government, didn't even own the land they worked."

He had studied the writings of Karl Marx, and he knew all about the Communist movement.

"They had the right idea," he said. "What we got in common is that we don't have anything. So we got nothing to lose. Once we all realize that, maybe something will happen."

"Are you saying it'll take a revolution, like they had in Russia?"

He thought about that for quite a while.

"I don't know," he said finally. "For sure they aren't going to give us anything. They never have. See, it's keepin' us down that keeps them up."

"Who's they?" I asked him.

"The rich and powerful people that keeps us under their thumbs," he said. "Hell, we should just reach up and bust them thumbs off and take what's comin' to us. There's a lot more of us than there are of them."

But he didn't think there would ever be a revolution like that in America.

"They're smart, see" he said. "They keep us divided, keep drivin' in wedges. That's why the poor whites hate us and, hell, man, we ain't hurtin' them. The enemies we got is the same ones they got. We oughta get together and take what's comin' to us, but how we gonna do that when they won't even let us shit in their toilets?"

A curious thing about Buck was that the more intellectual the ideas he was discussing, the more careless he became with syntax and grammar, and the more he sounded like Luke Redding, say, or Pete Simpson. Ordinarily he expressed himself very well, but when he got excited about some subject, when he cared the most, he slipped back into what many white people would have called "nigger talk." I have no idea why that was so.

"And when they push us too far, and it look like we might stop fightin' amongst ourselves and go after them, you know what they do then?" he asked.

"What?"

"They get a nice war goin' so as we got somebody else to fight. Oh, that always works. A lot of us get shipped off, and they is either dead or so miserable they forget how bad off they was before. Ones that stay home got lots of jobs, 'n make good money. Takes everybody's mind off the fact that they ain't nothin'. Oh, yeah, that works just fine."

"You really believe that?" I asked.

"Hell, yes," he said, "there's people like us killin' each

other right now in Spain, down there in Ethiopia, lots of places. That's how you get rid of poverty, man—kill off the poor people."

At other times he'd show his sense of humor, mostly about ironic things. One morning he, Cotton Nash and I were eating breakfast together in a field just outside of Chippewa Falls, Wisconsin. Sitting not far away was B.G. Stripped to the waist, his great gut hung out over his underwear shorts like chocolate brown lava from a volcano as he wolfed down a dozen or so eggs and a pound of bacon. He ate with his fingers, which were dripping with egg yolk and bacon fat, and once in a while he would wipe his mouth with the back of his hand.

"Now, there," Buck said, "is the most *grossest* man I have ever seen."

"I ain't gonna argue with you," Cotton said.

"Sweats more than it rains some years."

"Oughta be in a zoo."

"Farts like an elephant."

"Don't never wash, less he gets throwed into the river by a horse, which don't happen too often."

We kept our voices low as we said these things, of course, because B.G. could have polished off the three of us like so many more fried eggs—and with about equal enjoyment.

Buck and Cotton got talking about some of the catcher's legendary feats in putting away the groceries.

"One time down in Laredo I seen him eat twenty-two bowls of chili," Cotton said. "The real Texas red it was, too—hot enough to burn the ass off a polar bear. Maybe sixty-seventy pieces of toast along with it. Then come three whole pecan pies. And, shit, he still looked hungry when he was all done, I swear."

"Yessir," Buck agreed, "when it comes to eatin', we got us the black Babe Ruth right here."

We talked about the Bambino for a while—his tape measure home runs, his skinny legs and pot belly, his insatiable appetite for food, drink and women. Ruth had wound up as a coach with the Brooklyn Dodgers the year before, but was out of baseball by then. A couple of weeks earlier I had read about his appearance at Yankee Stadium to participate in the Appreciation Day they held for Lou Gehrig, the great first baseman who had been forced to quit because of a crippling illness. It had been a long article, more about Ruth than about "Iron Horse Lou."

"Did you know they used to call him 'Nigger' when he was a kid?" I asked them.

"Who?"

"The Babe. Got shortened to 'Nig' after a while."

"You shittin' us?" Cotton asked.

"No," I told him. "A lot of people say he's got some colored blood in him."

Suddenly Buck started to laugh.

"What's funny?" I asked him.

"Oh, shit, man—." He could hardly talk for laughing.

"What?"

"Oh, that's beautiful!"

I looked at him, still not knowing what he was getting at.

"They been so busy keepin' everything white," he said, the words coming out between spasms of laughter, "and all the time the Babe, their number one, all-time

111

hero—maybe he's part like us. Maybe the Babe is part nigger."

"I like that," Cotton said, and the two of us joined in Buck's laughter.

Cotton was probably the best ballplayer on the club. So quick around second base that his feet didn't seem to touch the ground like other people's, he could go to his left or right with equal ease. More than once I saw him move into the hole to cut off line shots that had zipped past the pitcher and bounced right over second base. And he had the pivot and the arm to turn such shots into outs. He was a great double play man, and at the plate it was hard to see how any pitcher could ever get him out. Not a power hitter, he used his thick, stubby bat to punch singles into left center and right center as regularly as the postman brings your mail.

Away from the diamond, Cotton stayed to himself most of the time, making no real enemies and having no real friends. He had been bitten by a cottonmouth down in Louisiana when he was nine years old. There wasn't a doctor within thirty miles, not a doctor that would take blacks anyway, and, although he recovered, one side of his face was still partly paralyzed. It was sometimes hard to tell whether he was smiling or scowling.

Like Buck, he was a very intelligent man and, also like Buck, Cotton was deeply aware that he was being cheated out of what should have been his because of his color. Although he was good at the reams, he resented having to do them more than any other All Star. He didn't read a great deal, and he wasn't a heavy thinker; what he felt welled up naturally from somewhere deep inside him, flowing from his heredity and the environ-

112

ment he had been born into, much as a wilderness spring is spawned by geological conditions that were created long before the first trickle of water ran between moss-covered rocks.

Cotton, I knew, would be a very bad man to have coming after you. If his hostility ever boiled out of him, the eruption would be violent and ruthless. Where Buck might contribute to the philosophy behind a rebellion of the poor and the oppressed, Cotton would be a hell of a good choice to lead the forces of revolution into battle. There, he would give and take no quarter. And you'd have to be crazy to bet that he wouldn't win.

He was just one of several All Stars who already carried hurts and wounds from the battle for survival to which they had been drafted from birth. Pete Simpson had lost his arm to a whirring saw in an Arkansas lumber mill when he was twelve years old and working that many hours a day for a buck-fifty a week.

"Took it off down here first," he told me, pointing to an imaginary place halfway between his wrist and his elbow. " 'Bout bled to death, I guess, but the worst time come when the poison got into it. Oh, it stunk somethin' awful."

"Was there a doctor to look after you?" I asked.

"No, no, not at first," Pete said. "Never had none 'round there, as I can recall. Got real bad after a while, and my daddy took me to Little Rock, to the hospital there."

He smiled and chuckled, seemingly in fond recollection of that time.

"Treated me real good, they did," he said. "Wasn't nothin' I couldn't have to eat, if I wanted it. Bacon 'n eggs, chicken, ice cream—only had to tell them, and there it would come."

He didn't appear to hold any grudge, or host any resentment.

"Lost the rest of it there, I did," he said, glancing toward the stump of his arm, a lost wing that would never know flight again.

"You blame anybody for what happened?" I asked him.

"Blame? Oh, no, it was a good man cut me. I'm 'holdin' to him."

Luke Redding, "the Gawk," had a bullet lodged somewhere in his abdomen. Latimore Lee said Luke's uncle had put it there, but he didn't know why.

Woodrow Wilson Jones had a jagged, ugly knife scar that ran from the lobe of his left ear, down his cheek and across under his mouth to the point of his chin.

"Beats lynchin', man," was all he would ever say about it.

# X

Looking back, it's hard to separate what you actually felt and understood during a particular time in your life from what you perhaps *should* have been able to see then, but which really only became clear through hindsight. I *think* I realized, that summer of 1939, that the likelihood of war was growing, day by day; in retrospect, there was a terrible inevitability in the succession of events reported by the newspapers and more personally dramatized by such radio commentators as Walter Winchell and H.V. Kaltenborn.

But, although there was a nagging, occasional awareness that the world, and everything familiar to me in it, might be running downhill, it all seemed very distant, like an earthquake in Paraguay; you could see the newsreels, and read about the thousands who were dead, and the many more who were homeless and disease-ridden and starving, and you knew it was all true, and you could be very sympathetic, but it was all happening in a place you had never seen, and it wasn't happening to you.

King George and Queen Elizabeth had come to Canada earlier that summer on some kind of centennial visit. There had been huge crowds and parades and pomp and circumstance and military reviews and unveilings and speeches about the British Empire and the might of the Royal Navy; and it had all seemed phony and boring and pretty silly.

I remember feeling much the same as a boy when I sometimes went to the Remembrance Day services that were held each November 11th in the park at the north end of the main street. The park backed onto the red brick and limestone block armories, and in summer the neatly kept flower beds with their geometric patterns and the stately old trees made it a pleasant, formally beautiful place. Cement walks crossed diagonally from corner to corner, curving around the war memorial where they intersected. The cenotaph had a stone base and, on top of it, two well-executed figures in greening and bird-stained metal: a young woman clutching an infant to her breast, and a soldier in battle dress standing guard over them. People who passed there—boys on roller-skates, men walking home from work with their lunch pails, young lovers—seldom so much as glanced at the war memorial; it was just part of the familiar scene, like the clock over the market hall.

It always seemed to be dark and depressing, and raw with cold, on November 11th. The leaves, so recently a youthful green, and more recently still red and yellow and golden in their maturity, lay sodden and dead on the greyish-brown grass. The bare branches made a funereal black lace against the lowering, dark clouds. The flower beds were dug up like so many oversize graves. The

116

whole world seemed ugly and resigned to waiting for the benediction of the year's first clean, white snow.

There would be two or three speeches, followed by some words of Scripture from one of the local ministers, and then everyone would stand in silence for sixty seconds, during which you could hear sounds from far away. Finally, a bugler would play "The Last Post," the notes sounding indescribably sad as they drifted out across the chill, barren scene.

But what I remember most vividly were the veterans, the "returned men." Most of them were in early middle age by then, though they seemed much older to me. Some were greying, some balding, some with pot bellies, many with glasses, and they did not look at all like soldiers any more. A great many of them wore blue serge suits that would otherwise be saved for Sundays, weddings and funerals. Rows of medals swayed and clanked together on their chests as they marched up to take their places in rows around the war memorial. I knew almost all of them by sight, and most of them by name; many were neighbors or fathers or uncles of friends of mine. A butcher, a lawyer, a baker, a doctor, a drunk, a printer, a window-cleaner. . . .

I realized, I understood, I accepted that they had gone overseas, lived like burrowing animals for months and years in the trenches, picked off lice and killed rats, shown incredible courage, walked over the putrefying corpses of their friends, gone in one side of hell and come out the other. But, growing older, they seemed such ordinary men, and I could not comprehend why they had offered up their young lives for abstract concepts like King and country, which couldn't have meant much

117

to them, and crossed an ocean to fight and die in an alien land to which they owed no real allegiance.

I was, in my boyhood, embarrassed by and for those ex-soldiers who formed ranks around the war memorial, and later on I just took it for granted that the world could never be so insane, or the young men so gullible, again.

And so, as the international situation went rapidly from bad to worse that summer of 1939, my thoughts were focused on other things—specifically, seeing Mary Lou Everett again, and my performance as a member of Chappie Johnson's Colored All Stars. I was counting the days until we returned to Hobblin, Minnesota. And I was trying to make it as a first baseman with one of the best ball clubs in all baseball.

I was reasonably satisfied with my play, both at the plate and in the field. I wasn't having too much trouble with the pitchers we faced, and only had one error in the first three or four weeks I was with the team. Anyway, they were plenty good enough to carry me, as to some extent they carried Pete Simpson and Sweetcorn. But, unlike our one-armed outfielder and our clown short-stop, I wasn't contributing much in the way of entertainment or comedy—just playing my position more or less adequately, and that was about all. I took part in the shadow ball, of course, which anybody could do, and Chappie had shown me a simple trick that I used a few times.

On a quick one- or two-hopper back to the mound, or to Cotton at second, the kind where the batter is going to be out by a country mile, I would take the throw and stand near the base, but not touching it. Until I finished the play, the runner had no choice but to keep coming.

I would wait and wait, and then just before his foot came down on the bag, I would flick out my toe and brush the corner of it.

The guy on the base path wasn't likely to be too amused, and the ream came dangerously close to the fine line between having fun with our opponents and making fun of them; but if the crowd was in a good mood, it was usually good for a laugh, and at least it got me into the act once in a while.

For the most part I was strictly a straightman, and it bothered me some, even if it didn't seem to bother the others, that I wasn't pulling my full share of the weight.

No matter how many times I saw them, I still laughed without fail at some of the things they did, and continued to marvel at others.

Apart from his regular reams, Sweetcorn had a great natural instinct for seeing the humor in a particular situation, and milking it for all it was worth. One night in Mansfield, Ohio, the local shortstop booted two routine ground balls in a row, much to the chagrin of the hometown crowd.

Suddenly Sweetcorn was running out onto the field, carrying his glove, and hollering in his shrill voice.

"Now, don't you worry none! Sweetcorn is comin!"

He positioned himself beside and just behind the unfortunate shortstop.

"You be all right now. We gonna do it *together.*"

Playing his part, the next All Star hitter chopped the first pitch toward them on the ground.

Sweetcorn started jumping around, moving in and moving out, and the shortstop ran this way and that totally confused.

"I got it," Sweetcorn yelled. "No, no, you take it. My ball. You the shortstop. Look out! We got it."

The ball dribbled through their four legs and out into left center. Immediately, Sweetcorn ran over and confronted the second baseman.

"Why didn't you take it, man? You *seen* we was in trouble, me and him!"

And, as they argued, the runner took second, which was uncovered at the time.

The crowd, of course, ate it up.

Another time, in another town, it had rained all day and continued to drizzle as the game got underway, by which time the field was like a swamp. About the third inning Sweetcorn hit a single into shallow right, which he tried to stretch into a double by sliding headfirst into second. But there was a big pool of water on the base path, and it turned out be more of a dive than a slide. Finding his forward motion stopped about eight feet short of the bag, Sweetcorn began to swim for it with exaggerated dog-paddle motions.

The umpire, not impressed, called him out as Sweetcorn got to his feet, dripping wet.

"Maybe I out," he shrieked, "but I ain't drowned."

We used a lot of firecrackers to spice things up. You could still buy torpedoes then, which went off on impact, and B.G. would sometimes slip one into his catcher's mitt when Luke Redding was really throwing smoke. The loud bang was guaranteed to scare hell out of any local hotshot who already knew he wasn't going to hit Luke if he lived to be five hundred. Or somebody would sneak out and drop a string of ladyfingers at the plate umpire's feet; the fans always loved to see the man in blue dance.

To open proceedings each night, maybe a half-hour before game time, B.G., Buck and Woodrow Wilson Jones would walk out to home plate, each carrying a fungo bat and a ball. In unison, they would toss the balls up in the air and hit all three of them out of the park. They'd do it casually, as if they were just testing out the place; but, no matter how big the ball park, those balls would go out of there like so many skyrockets—one over the left field fence, one in deep center, and one in right.

That was enough to intimidate any hometown ball club, right there.

One routine I always liked was used when we had men on first and second, and the batter singled to left or left center field. As soon as the ball was safely out of the infield, while all eyes were on the base hit, whoever was coaching at first would take off for second ahead of the legitimate runner—thus giving us four guys on the base paths instead of three. The man on second would score easily, so that the only possible play would be at third base. The first base coach would time it so that he would be thrown out there. Then he would jump up, shouting and pointing to second base.

"No, no, it ain't me you want. That's him, back there!"

The umpires would scratch their heads until they finally noticed that the first base coaching box was empty. Then they would have a long conference and consult their rule books, and usually come to the conclusion that there wasn't much they could do about it. In the confusion, the runners generally managed to steal third and second.

Apart from me, everybody on the club had at least one

pet ream or specialty. Cotton often threw behind his back to me, and a few times he and Sweetcorn even teamed up for double plays that way. B.G. might catch an inning with his bare hands. Pete Simpson caught fly balls between his legs. Buck would hit a half-dozen line drives in a row over the left field fence, just foul, and then rifle the seventh one out fair.

One night I mentioned to Chappie that I'd like to work out something I could do. We were sitting in some dugout, waiting for the local team to finish infield practice.

"Forget it, Joe," he said. "You gettin' along just fine."

"Maybe, but I'd like to try."

"So you want a ream."

"Yeah."

He glanced along the bench. "Malachi, you come over here a minute?"

The third baseman joined us, sitting on the other side of Chappie.

"What I done now?" he asked.

"Nothin' I know 'bout," Chappie said. "You think you might play a little 'ain't lookin' with Joe, here?"

Malachi shrugged, but looked faintly pleased. "Sure," he said, "long as he's willin'."

"You think he can handle it?" Chappie asked. There was a kind of seriousness about the way he put the question.

Malachi thought it over. "He ain't got no wife or kids, has he?" he asked.

"No," Chappie told him.

"Oughta be all right, then," Malachi said.

"How does it work?" I asked.

"Just gotta stand there, is all," Malachi said.

122

"Thank you, Mr. Brown," Chappie said.

"That's okay." Malachi went back to where he'd been sitting.

"What's 'ain't lookin'?" I asked Chappie.

"Easier to show than tell," Chappie told me. "We'll try it out, first chance comes along."

Grateful for Chappie's approval, but still curious, I asked Buck about it later that night on the bus.

" 'Ain't lookin' '?" he answered. "Oh, that's a real good ream."

"Yeah?"

"When it comes off," he added.

"It's hard, eh?"

"Well, you know," he said, "it takes time to work out a ream."

"I guess so," I said.

" 'Course, the trouble with 'ain't lookin'," he said, "is that you don't usually get a second chance."

"Why not?"

"Forget it," Buck said. "I shouldn't have said anything. No sense in getting all worked up before the time comes."

"Tell me," I said. "I want to know."

He hesitated for a few moments, as though searching his mind for just the right words.

"You ever been kicked by a horse?" he asked finally. "Where the kidneys are?"

"Of course not," I told him.

"Well, don't worry," he said, "it'll probably be all right."

"What the hell do you mean, 'don't worry'?" I demanded.

But he had switched off his light, and was already asleep—or pretending to be. I sat for another hour or so in the darkness, wondering why I hadn't been content to leave well enough alone.

The following day, about four or five in the afternoon, we were driving along the edge of a town, on our way to wherever we were scheduled to play that night, when Chappie told B.G., who was at the wheel of the bus, to pull over and stop. There was a ball diamond just off the road, deserted in the hot sun, with weeds encroaching on the bumpy infield path and a sagging, chicken-wire backstop behind home plate.

"Malachi, Joe—you ready?" Chappie asked.

Malachi was already moving up the aisle, his glove tucked under his arm.

"What for?" I asked.

" 'Ain't lookin', what else?" Chappie said.

"Oh, sure."

The three of us went across the road, through some tall grass, and around the end of the screen onto the ball field. I knew that the others who had stayed on the bus were watching.

"Come over here, Joe," Chappie said, and led the way to the first base area. It was as rough around there as ice on a pond in late March. He peeled off his windbreaker, and dropped it on the dusty, bare earth.

"That'll be the bag," he said. "Now, I want you to stand like this." He took a position facing away from the diamond, looking 180 degrees in the other direction.

I did as he said. It seemed strange, having my back to the diamond.

"How's that?" I asked.

"Fine, just fine," he said, coming around in front of me. "I'm goin' in, and hit one down to Malachi. Start countin' when you hear the bat meet the ball."

"Okay."

"Get to seven, put your glove 'round behind, like this." He held his hand, the pinkish-black palm outwards, in the small of his back, about waist high.

"Then what?" I asked.

"Just wait, is all," Chappie said, "and don't move."

Suddenly, it became clear; I was supposed to trust Malachi to hit a target, maybe eight inches round, from the far corner of the diamond, a hundred or so feet away. If he missed, I could wind up pissing blood or in a wheelchair.

"You ready?" Chappie asked.

"Oh, sure," I said, wishing I had been born with some brains.

He went away, and I stood there, staring out across fields of maturing corn. It seemed to take him a hell of a long time to reach the plate. I waited . . . and waited. Maybe the ream was that he and Malachi had got back on the bus, leaving me to dangle there like some kind of ass-backward scarecrow.

Finally I heard the sound of bat on ball, and I started counting—one . . . two . . . three. . . . When I got to seven I slipped my right hand, cocooned by the big first base mitt, around behind and held it hard against my belt. Another year or so of my life ticked away. Trickles of sweat ran down my forehead. I strained to spread my thumb and fingers, making the pocket as wide as possible. In the kidneys, Buck had said. Jesus! I winced, anticipating the pain.

125

Suddenly a bomb exploded in my right hand, the shock of it travelling up my arm, through my shoulder and neck, and into my head. Instinctively, the nerve hinge in my glove snapped shut, and I somehow held onto the throw. A few seconds later I turned around slowly, trying to keep my knees from shaking.

Chappie was coming out along the first base line, holding up his empty hand for the ball as if what had just happened was a routine thing.

"Let's do it another time," was all he said.

We did it again, and after that another four or five times. I dropped the ball once out of nervousness, but it was unfailingly on target, somewhere in the long trough-shaped pocket between the end of my thumb and the heel of the glove. After the first two or three tries I was able to judge pretty well when the ball would arrive, and that made it easier. Physically, any half-decent first baseman should have been able to catch a thousand in a row. The challenge was psychological; it was hard standing there with your back turned, not knowing what was going on behind you—and hard too to have enough confidence in Malachi, to believe that anybody could be that good. If just one of those throws sailed so much as six inches on a vagrant current of air, or was just a shade off-line.... Ordinarily, of course, you could adjust to any changes in the flight of the ball, compensating, shifting your glove, your stance, your whole body; but in 'ain't lookin' ' there was no margin for error.

"You figure you can do it in a game now?" Chappie asked after we got back on the bus. My teammates, having watched the workout with such sadistic interest, had given no indication that they were impressed by it; even

126

Buck, damn him, pretended he was asleep.

"Sure," I said, "how do we set it up?"

"Fifth innin'," he said. "I'll get our guy to let up a little and throw inside to righties. That oughta get us a grounder down third. Ain't the fifth, maybe the sixth."

"Okay," I told him. "One thing, though."

"Uh-huh."

"What am I supposed to be looking at out there away from the field?"

Chappie shrugged. "Don't matter," he said. "Bird flyin', maybe an airoplane, little kids playin', whatever you see."

"Won't I look pretty stupid?" I asked.

"You is *supposed* to look stupid," Chappie said, his voice a little impatient. "You wanted a ream, and lookin' stupid is part of this one."

"All right," I said.

"Don't forget you is a dumb nigger now," he told me. "Be ready when they come up in the fifth."

We played that night in Bloomington, Indiana. A college town, it seemed almost deserted in mid-summer.

"You could shoot a machine gun 'round this town, 'n not hit nothin' but a couple of dogs," Latimore Lee said as we drove through the near empty streets.

Still, eight or nine hundred showed up for the game that night, a lot of them farmers from the surrounding countryside.

"Be ready," Chappie told me as we ran out for the home team's half of the fifth.

As soon as I had taken the warm-up throws from the other infielders, I turned my back on the diamond and stared out past the corner of the left field grandstand, doing my best to look as if I was fascinated by something that had caught my eye. To tell the truth, there was nothing out there except a couple of houses, a few trees and a hell of a lot of corn. I kept peering and staring, though, like I was expecting King Kong to come into view at any second.

Every now and then I'd sneak a quick look out of the corner of my eye to see what was happening in the ball game behind me. Unfortunately, that wasn't much; the first two batters popped up to Sweetcorn, and the third struck out, even though Luke Redding was laying the ball in there as soft and gentle as a wooly lamb.

By the end of the inning some of the fans on the first base side were laughing, and a few were beginning to get on me.

"Hey, Sambo, you're missin' a good ball game!"

"Look behind you—yoo-hoo, turn around!"

"You there on first, they went thataway!"

I kept it up when they came up in the sixth. The fans were looking for it by then, and the heckling started right away. The first pitch was a called strike, and then I heard the bat make contact with the ball. I glanced around just enough to see the batter looking down the third base line as he dropped his bat and dug in for first.

This is it, I thought, as I started counting. Three . . . four . . . five . . . six . . . seven. The runner was about ten feet away, and coming hard. Close play. A lot of the fans were screaming at me to turn around. The throw must be almost there.

At the last moment I put my glove behind my back, spreading the pocket over my belt. The count might have gone to eight, perhaps nine ... and then, wham, the ball was there. Perfect, right on the money! My fingers snapped over it, and at the same instant I flicked out my toe and touched the corner of the bag. The umpire jerked his arm up, and the guy was out by a step or so. Close all right.

Then, suddenly, I was aware of the crowd. Some of the fans were laughing, others clapping, a few whistling. They loved it! The applause was for me, and I loved that —although it should have been for Malachi.

Eating it up, I swung my glove toward the stands in a kind of informal salute, then threw to Cotton to start the ball on its way around the horn.

Free to go into high gear again, Luke Redding struck out the next batter on three pitches to retire the side.

Approaching the dugout I caught up to Malachi, who was never known to run when he could walk, or walk when he could sit down.

"Thanks," I told him, "I really appreciate it."

"Should, too," he said, "and remember to be good to old Malachi from here on. He just might get careless one time."

The days and nights of that July passed one by one, and the bus and truck rolled on, criss-crossing state lines —North Dakota, Minnesota, Wisconsin, Illinois, Indiana, Michigan, Ohio, then swinging back north and west again.

Each day a new town, every night a different ball park. And, if the All Stars did not really look the least bit alike, the towns were carbon copies of one another. I remember some of the ball parks, however—one where right field climbed a hill, another where the base paths were red (because of iron in the soil, someone said)—but the towns were just so many dots on a series of folded road maps.

The same thing with time. Dates didn't mean much, and it came as surprise when I discovered that we had somehow turned the corner and moved into August. On Saturdays the main streets of the towns would be crowded with farmers in for market, weekly shopping and haircuts, and sometimes there would be the sound of church bells on a Sunday morning; otherwise, I seldom gave a thought to the day of the week.

We travelled hundreds and hundreds of miles, but never really saw much; and I'd already had my fill of staring across meaningless countryside, other people's countryside, from the open doors of empty freight cars. Nobody was ever broadened much by that kind of travel. Toughened, maybe, but not broadened. The endless hours we spent in the confined, crowded, smelly prison that was the bus could only be endured by putting your mind into a state of suspension between sleep and wakefulness, or by finding a way of escape. Some played poker. Buck read. Latimore Lee sang songs under his breath that only he understood. Chappie kept his accounts.

We ate a lot of greasy food, meat that was undercooked, vegetables that had had the life boiled out of them, stale bread, watery soup, pieces of pie that had been walked over by a hundred flies.

We hardly ever got a decent night's sleep, as most of the time we had to cramp our too long bodies into the too narrow seats of the bus. Though once in a while we lay down in the open, contoured to the grass and bare earth, under the stars and drifting clouds and sudden, cold rain.

It was a little better in states like Illinois, Ohio and Michigan, where there were a lot of blacks, because even though the prejudice was stronger, and you had to keep looking over your shoulder, the rules were more clear-cut. There were places you didn't go, things you didn't do; but Chappie knew a Negro cafe here or lunch counter there where we could get a decent meal; and three or four times we even got to sleep between clean sheets in hotels run by colored people.

I soon grew to hate the lighting equipment. The others hated it too, and some of them had for years. It wasn't hard work, but the monotony grated on your nerves; the same thing every night—put it up, take it down, put it up, take it down. The fact that it was such a practiced, almost orchestrated routine just made it worse, even if it was efficient and never failed to impress the fans who arrived early enough to see us go through it. Each player had a specific role to play in the scenario; mine was to erect the light standard back of first base, and plug in the leading and outgoing cables. I went through those steps so often that the first thing I used to think about some mornings was that damn, flimsy tower and how I would have to put it together again that night. The record for stringing the whole lighting system, and throwing the generator switch that would bring the rows of 100-watt bulbs to life, was fourteen minutes and thirty seconds; we never even came close to that while I was with the All Stars.

A lot of things were difficult. Laundry, for one. There never was a washing machine available, nor any hot water; we scrubbed our socks, shirts, shorts and uniforms in rivers and roadside ponds, and often hung them out the bus windows to dry. We shaved in water so hard that you couldn't get a lather, and had to scrape off the whiskers with a bare razor blade. There was no mail, because we had no address. The only privacy came when it was your turn to drive the bus.

In many ways we were like prisoners in a touring jail, cooped up for countless hours, cut off from the rest of the world, freed once a day to put on our show, then herded back into our communal cell.

Yet it wasn't bad. There were the shared experiences, and there was a camaraderie and a kind of unspoken, common loyalty.

Most of all, I liked playing ball every night—liked it better than anything I had ever done or known. I liked the sights and sounds of the game. I liked the more or less crowded stands. I liked the looseness. I liked the slap of the ball when it nestled into the pocket of my glove, and the solid tingle in my hands and wrists when I got good wood on a fast ball. I never tired of watching Cotton Nash go to his right, backhand the ball and flip it in one fluid motion to Sweetcorn to start a zip-zip double play. I liked the geometric perfection of the diamond, even when the chalk lines were wobbly, the outfield was riddled with gopher holes, and the base paths were chewed away by encroaching weeds. The laughs. The chatter. B.G. setting his target. Latimore Lee coming in with his high, hard one. Buck Yancey, drifting away under a well-hit fly ball, and turning at the last moment to make the catch over his shoulder at the base of the centerfield fence. The umpires, maybe not always right, but never wrong. The excitement. The action. The perfection. The errors.

The game.

I was well aware that I was no better than a Class 'C' first baseman, lucky enough to be playing with a bunch of guys who, by every right, should have been in the majors. Under the circumstances, though, I didn't think I was hurting the ball club. My new ream had given me more confidence, and I added a few other little gimmicks that contributed to the comedy part of the show.

Chappie seemed satisfied. Otherwise, I told myself, he would have sent for a replacement; the All Stars meant too much to him to put up with an inadequate performance. He was a proud man. To make sure, though, I put it to him directly one noon when he and I were waiting for a garage mechanic to put new brake linings in the truck. The others were camped a couple of miles out of the town. Chappie and I were sitting in the shade of a chestnut tree, from where we could see the truck up on the hoist with its rear wheels off. As usual by then, I was wearing the lampblack under my ball cap.

"Mr. Johnson," I asked, "you think things are going all right?"

He thought about it for a moment, then nodded.

"Sure," he said, "good as anybody could expect. Just get them new linings in, we be laughin'."

"I meant me," I told him.

He looked surprised. "You itchin' to move on?" he asked.

"No."

"You gettin' along, ain't you?"

"With the others?"

133

"Uh-huh."

"I think so," I said.

"I ain't hearin' no complaints," he said.

"That's good."

"Stay a spell then, if you want," he said.

"I'd like to," I told him.

He leaned back on his elbows, and looked up at the white chestnut blossoms.

"You fieldin' as good as anybody I could bring in," he said.

"Thanks."

He laughed. " 'Course you should be," he said, "on account of I taught you all I knows."

I laughed too. "How about hitting?" I asked him.

"Shit," he said, "Chappie'd hit .400 down here, and I is fifty-four years old."

"You would, at that," I said.

He glanced over toward the garage.

"Looks like we got wheels again," he said. "Let's get goin'."

"Thanks, Chappie," I said.

"Mr. Johnson," he reminded me.

The next night after that we played a town called Appleton in Wisconsin. We had a good feeling about the place as we turned in off the highway. Clean streets. Recently mowed lawns and flower beds around substantial looking, freshly painted houses. A nice park in front of the court house. Progressive. Pleasant. Friendly. A nice town.

It was the same at the ball park, two or three hours later. The infield path had been raked, our dugout had been swept clean of popcorn boxes, chocolate bar and chewing gum wrappers, crumpled cigarette packages. The fans started to file in well before game time, and they kept coming. You could sense that they were in a good mood, and had come to be entertained. The kind of crowd that makes you want to do your best.

Everything went fine for five innings. We trotted out all of our top reams. The crowd oohed and aahed, laughed and applauded. The local players were easygoing and didn't take losing too hard; maybe they had had a lot of practice.

Then, in their half of the fifth, disaster showed its ugly face in Appleton. There was no warning that all hell was about to break loose. I set up "ain't lookin' " to start the inning, and was staring off toward the south, watching a big, lumbering crow being chased by a posse of smaller birds, probably swallows. The first batter obligingly hit a soft three-hopper down to Malachi. I started the count and, when I got to seven, put the glove around behind at my belt. The ball was there, as always. Smack! The umpire started his 'out' motion. The fans began to rumble their appreciation.

Strictly routine; Malachi and I had done it again.

Then the breath was knocked out of me, and I was turning ass over tea kettle on the grass. The batter had plowed into me but, even as I rolled, I knew it wasn't his fault. Hell, I'd been standing right on the bag. Careless. He'd just been trying to beat it out, like any decent ballplayer would do. I hurt some, but the ball was still in my glove and I came up laughing. No problem.

Well, there *was* one; my ball cap had been knocked off in the collision. Suddenly I was the world's first and only brown-haired, blue-eyed Negro first baseman. I heard a

135

buzz running through the crowd, a hum of surprise and shock.

"Look, they got a white guy playin' first!"

"Well, by damn . . ."

"Never seen the like of it!"

It wasn't an angry sound, though. The fans seemed more intrigued than annoyed, and ready to see the humor in the situation.

"What's the matter, Chappie—you run outa niggers?"

"How many more whites you got out there?"

Typically, Sweetcorn picked that up right away. He ran in to a spot about half-way between the pitcher's mound and home plate. There he stopped, doffed his cap, and did a kind of pirouette as he swept it gracefully in front of him. As he did this he bent down to give everybody a full view of his head of kinky and very black hair.

"Ain't no white on Sweetcorn," he hollered. "Ain't no white on me."

The fans laughed, liking it, and the other All Stars took it from there. One by one, starting with Malachi, they spun around, pointing to their hair.

"I black all over."

While this was going on, I retrieved my cap and pulled it down over my brown hair. By then the laughter was solid all around me. When play finally resumed, Latimore got the inning over with as quickly as possible, striking out the next two hitters on six pitches. B.G. put a torpedo in his mitt to punctuate the last one. The fans gave us a big hand as we came in off the field. When we got to the dugout I looked over to where Chappie almost always sat, in the corner closest to home plate. He was laughing too.

136

I went over to him.

"You want me to come out?" I asked.

The laughter drained out of his face as if I had pulled the plug.

"Come out?" he asked.

"I don't mind," I told him. "It was my fault."

"What in the world you want to do that for?" He started laughing again. "Hell, that's maybe the best ream I ever did see. Oh, my!"

The laughter was contagious.

"It was pretty good at that, wasn't it?"

"I think—" he said, tears coming into his eyes, "I think we gonna do it every night!"

That wouldn't have been possible, of course, because the fans in a lot of towns would have felt cheated by a white guy masquerading as a colored ball player. But nobody in Appleton seemed upset over it.

Or hardly anybody.

We gave the crowd a good show for the remaining innings, and got a lot of applause when the game was over. The fans were filtering out through the exits and we were gathering up the gear, when we heard a voice from the dugout steps.

"You there, boy, what's your name?"

I glanced up and saw the figure of a big man, silhouetted against the lights. He was wearing a sheriff's uniform, and I caught the glint of a star on the left front of his short-sleeved shirt. There was a gun in a holster on his belt. And he was looking right at me.

"Who?"

"You know who."

The months on the road had taught me that you never

got anywhere by antagonizing a police officer, but this one's overbearing manner and sneering voice made that hard to remember. He came down the rest of the way into the dugout, and he *was* big. Young—early thirties, I guessed. Handsome in a hard way. Slim hipped, but with the upper body of a football guard or tackle.

"My name's Joe Giffen," I told him.

The others had stopped what they were doing, and were watching intently.

He nodded, smiled—but not with his eyes.

"That's a good boy, Joe," he said. "Now, I want you to just come along with me, nice and easy."

"What?"

"Nothin' complicated about it," he said. "I'm takin' you in, is all."

Chappie pushed his way past B.G. and Malachi to stand beside me.

"You mind tellin' me what the charge is, officer?" he asked.

"Who the hell are you?" the sheriff asked.

"This here's one of my ballplayers," Chappie told him.

"Uh-huh," the sheriff said, "well, we got a choice on him."

"Like what?" Chappie asked.

"Oh, take fraud, for instance. Cheatin' the public. Then there's impersonatin' a nigger—unlawfully."

"Impersonating a nigger!" Buck said, behind me. "Holy Jesus!"

"What do you want me to do, Mr. Johnson?" I asked.

"Don't seem like there's too much choice," Chappie said. "Best go along with it. I'll be down soon as I can." He looked up at the sheriff, who was a head taller than

138

he was, and maybe a hundred pounds heavier. "Where's he gonna be at?" he asked.

"County jail," the big man said. "Real nice. Hearin' is set for tomorrow mo'nin'."

"All right."

"Then let's haul ass," the sheriff said.

I walked beside him along in front of the stands, across a parking area and out through the main gate. He kept blowing bubbles with the big wad of gum he was chewing. The last few fans were still on their way out, and some of them looked over, curiosity in their eyes.

There was a yellow and blue squad car parked at the curb. The sheriff opened the back door and got in after me. His deputy turned around from the steering wheel.

"Where to, Roy?" he asked.

"Oh, shit" the sheriff said, "where do you think? You wanta buy him some ribs out at Porky's?"

"I was just askin'," the deputy said.

"Well, don't ask," the sheriff told him.

It took us about fifteen minutes to get there. The county jail was a square, limestone-block appendage behind a graceful, red-brick courthouse that looked as if it had been there forever.

The sheriff picked up a ring of big keys from a nail in his office, and led the way through a heavy oak door and along a short corridor. There were bars on either side, and it was like a dungeon under the high ceiling. He stopped in front of the second cell on the right and unlocked the door. It squeaked as he opened it, then clanged solidly shut behind me.

"You'll be just fine here," the sheriff said as he turned away. "Have a good night now, y' hear?"

Oh, sure.

The place reeked of strong disinfectant, which was trying, with only limited success, to overcome the smells of urine, sweat, vomit and mildew. A bare, fly-specked light bulb burned overhead. There was a stool at one end, a bucket and a steel bunk with a straw mattress at either side, in one of which was sprawled the body of a man. He didn't move once while I was there, and I never did know whether he was dead drunk or just dead.

It's hard to describe how I felt. Not scared, actually. Not apprehensive, particularly. Mostly, the whole thing seemed unreal. And kind of funny. I stood by the cell door, my hands grasping the bars, and wondered what the hell was going to happen.

An hour went by, maybe two. Then I heard footsteps, and saw the deputy approaching. He was carrying a paper bag in one hand, the ring of keys in the other. It took a minute or so of fumbling to get the cell door open, after which he held out the paper bag to me.

"Here."

"What's this?" I asked.

"Ribs," he said. "Your nigger friend figured you might be hungry."

"From Porky's?"

"How'd you know?" he said.

The ribs were good—tender, meaty, smothered in a tangy, sweet sauce. I stripped the bones clean, along with a carton of potato salad, a toasted roll and a paper cup of coffee. Thank you, Chappie. Then, feeling pretty good considering my predicament, I went over and curled up on the other mattress.

I woke up feeling like a skinny old bear in March. I was stiff, a lot of muscles ached, and my mouth tasted like second base. Sunlight was coming through the only window, high up in one wall. The sheriff himself was rattling the bars with a spoon.

"You want your breakfast, you better come and get it," he said.

I stretched, rolled off the mattress, and went over to the cell door. He handed me a mug of lukewarm coffee, and a tin plate, on which some watery, greyish-green scrambled eggs had drowned a piece of toast sometime during the night.

"Thanks a lot," I told him.

"Don't be too long," he said. "Court sits in forty minutes."

"You suppose I could wash up before that?" I asked.

He took a step backwards, as if I had called his sister a whore, but quickly recovered.

"Oh no, smart ass," he said, "there won't be no destroyin' evidence. I want you in there just the way you was."

He went away, and I sat on the edge of the bunk and drank some of the coffee. I put the scrambled eggs on the floor by the other bunk, in case my cell-mate should revive, which seemed increasingly unlikely.

The sheriff came back in about half an hour and took me out of the jail, across a small yard under some big old oak trees, and through a side door into the courtroom. Outside, the sun was bright, and everything—trees, lawn, flowers, courthouse—looked freshly washed.

By contrast, it was cool and hushed in the courtroom. Only a dozen or so people, including the sheriff and me, were on hand to witness the case of *The State of Wisconsin*

v. *Joseph Giffen*. The court reporter was a nice looking, middle-aged woman in a floral housedress. The Assistant District Attorney, a pudgy young man in his early thirties, had a lingering case of acne. Chappie, wearing his All Star windbreak, was sitting in the front row. Six or seven spectators, there for God knows what reasons, were scattered around in the polished-wood, churchlike pews.

Circuit Court Judge Wilbur Clay Calhoun couldn't have been a day under eighty, nor a fraction of an inch over five foot two. His face was thin and deeply lined under a fringe of closed-cropped, grey hair, and he looked so frail that it was hard to believe there was a body beneath the folds of his shiny blue serge suit. When he glanced down at me through his rimless glasses, I got the impression that he had given up smiling some years before.

The sheriff indicated that I was to sit at a small oak table below the bench, and as soon as I had taken my place the trial got under way. The Assistant D.A. led off. He stuttered pretty badly from time to time, but I got the idea that I was being charged with fraud and false pretenses for pretending to be a black ballplayer when I was really white.

The sheriff took the stand and testified that he had arrested me the previous night after my ball cap had been accidentally knocked off. The Assistant D.A. introduced into evidence one of the posters that had been put up around Appleton, announcing that the 'Colored All Stars' were coming to town.

"I su—su—submit, Your Honor, that the clear im—im—imp—implication of this placard is that all of the players are of the nig—Negro race. And I ask that it be marked as Ex—Ex—Exhibit 'A'."

"No need to get fancy, Henry," the judge told him. "Just put it there on the table. Let me have a look at it first, though, will you?"

He studied it at arms length for a minute or so, then just kind of pushed it off the front of the bench. The court reporter in the floral dress went over, picked it up, and put it on the table.

"Thank you, Martha," the judge said.

At that point Chappie stood up.

"Your Honor, may I say somethin'?" he asked.

"Who are you?" Judge Calhoun wanted to know.

"I runs the All Stars," Chappie said.

"Oh, you do, eh?"

"Yessir, and I just wanted to say that we didn't mean no harm. We try to play good and make people laugh, that's all. Joe, here, he part of the team, like everybody else."

"I object!" the Assistant D.A. said, leaping to his feet.

"To what?" the judge asked him.

"This—this man has no o—o—official ca—ca- cap—capacity, and I . . ."

"Now, Henry," the judge said, grimacing as he interrupted, "this is not exactly the Lindbergh kidnapping trail we have here. I think we can afford to be a little informal."

"But, but . . ."

"Sit down, Henry," the judge said, turning back to look toward Chappie.

"Mr. Johnson," he said, "you've been around baseball for quite a spell, is that right?"

"Oh, I didn't come by just yesterday," Chappie told him.

"Neither did I," His Honor said. "Now, tell me how you came to hire this player for your team."

Chappie explained how it had happened.

"Uh-huh," the judge said when he was finished. "So you could say that it was a matter of being in the right place at the right time?"

"Yessir," Chappie agreed, "you could say that."

"And it saved you money."

"You could say that, too," Chappie told him.

"All right," the judge said. He looked over at me. "I'd like to ask the defendant a question or two."

The sheriff leaned across the table. "On your feet, boy," he said. I got up.

"Tell me," His Honor said, peering down through his glasses, "are you a good ballplayer?"

"I'm all right," I said, "but not as good as some of the others."

"Not as good as Mickey Cochrane, for instance?"

"No, sir, not as good as Malachi or Buck either."

"I always appreciate modesty," the judge said. "There's so little of it. Can you play the bag?"

"Yes, sir."

"Hit?"

"As long as I don't see too many good curve balls."

"Do you see too many?"

"No, sir, not against the teams we play."

"Do you help to entertain the fans?"

"Well, I think so, now that I got my own ream. . . ."

"Your own what?"

I told him about 'ain't lookin'.

"I see," the judge said. "What's that stuff on your face?"

"It's called lampblack," I told him.

"Oh, yes, of course. Well, that will be all, I think. You can sit down now."

He looked over at the Assistant D.A.

"Henry," he said, "I hope you won't consider this out of order . . ."

Henry jumped up.

"Anything you s—s—say, Your Honor."

"Thank you. Would you be good enough to name some colors for me?"

"S—s—some what?"

"Some colors, Henry—you know, like we all learn in grade school."

"Oh, sure," Henry said. "Well, there's green and blue and o—o—orange and brown and pink . . ."

"You're doing just fine, Henry," the judge said. "Keep going."

". . . and white and purple and red and black . . ."

"Ah, yes, black," the judge interrupted. "Now, Henry, take a good look at the defendant's face. How would you describe it, as far as the hue is concerned?"

"W—we—well, it's kind of black, but he just rubbed it on. . . ."

"And black is a color? You said so yourself."

"Oh, d—d—damn!"

Judge Calhoun turned to face me and Chappie and the almost empty benches of his courtroom.

"The advertisement used by the All Stars doesn't say anything about how they got to be 'Colored,' " he said, "but only specifies that they are. The sun is shining and

145

it's a nice day outside. I think we have all wasted enough time."

He picked up his gavel and banged it down three or four times on the bench.

"The defendant is found *not guilty*," he said. "Court stands adjourned."

# IX

Since there had been no way of knowing how long we might be held up in Appleton, the others had gone on ahead, with Malachi in charge as acting manager. About two o'clock that afternoon Chappie and I got on a bus that would catch up with the ball club in time for the game that night. I still had the lampblack on, and the uniform, which was beginning to smell a little ripe. Chappie wasn't too sure about the segregation laws in Wisconsin, so we shared a seat near the back; no sense in asking for trouble when we were feeling so good about how things had turned out in the courtroom.

We talked about that most of the way.

"That man," Chappie said once, wonderment in his voice, "now there was a real human bein'. I liked him some."

"Me too," I agreed.

"Uh-huh," Chappie said.

We had to describe everything that had happened, in

147

full detail, when we rejoined the All Stars that evening. Chappie did most of the talking. When he was finished, the others were clustered around, laughing with us.

"I wished I'd been there, man," Cotton said.

"Oh, yeah!"

It was then, while we were laughing about the trial and getting ready to play the Eau Claire (Wisconsin) Tigers, that I got my nickname—an event that was more important than it sounds.

The survival of the ball club depended on two very different kinds of humor. On the one hand there was the clown stuff—the slapstick, the gags, the kind of comedy that Sweetcorn was so good at. That was necessary to bring the fans into the ball parks, and it was all most people ever saw.

Funny niggers.

But if the All Stars made people laugh at them, they also laughed at and among themselves. That was their private laughter. The humor behind it was subtle, usually ironic, often bitter. It was a defense against the injustices and indignities they had to endure every day of their lives.

"You laughs or you cries," Chappie said.

The shelter provided by that humor was a shared thing, a secret thing, a protected thing. One element of it was that each of the All Stars had a nickname—one that was never used in public, but only among themselves. In that inner sanctum, B.G. was called "Meat"; Peter Simpson was "Stumpy"; Buck Yancey was "Books"; Malachi was "Little Cool"; Latimore Lee was the "Gawk."

And, by the time we took the field that night in Eau

148

Claire, I had become "Cap" Giffen. It was Buck who started it.

"You were sure some lucky," he said.

"Since when is it lucky to spend a night in jail?" I asked him.

"Well, I'll tell you, Cap," he said. "If this was Mississippi, and they'd got you for impersonatin' a white man, you'd have been gone for maybe a hundred an' ninety-two years."

"The man's got it right," Cotton laughed.

"Wouldn't catch me playin' for no *white* All Stars," Sweetcorn added. "No sir, Cap, not me!"

It stuck from then on, and it mattered to me because it meant that I had been accepted, not just as a fringe ballplayer, but as a member of the team, the group. Like "Meat" and the "Gawk," it was part of a private, insular world into which I had been adopted.

Joe "Cap" Giffen; I felt good about that.

# *XII*

A couple of days later we were on the final leg back to Hobblin, home of Mary Lou Everett, whom I was determined to see again in spite of Chappie's warning. It wasn't going to be easy, though, unless we got rained out a second time.

Forget that; as we rolled toward Duluth, where we would cross over into Minnesota, there wasn't a cloud in the early afternoon sky. It looked like it might never spit a drop of rain again.

Well, at least we were going to get there with plenty of time to spare; I'd get in touch with her somehow and set something up for after the game.

Forget that too.

About two o'clock, still an hour or so south and east of Duluth, the bus suddenly started wandering back and forth across the highway like a drunken miner on pay night. Cotton, who was at the wheel, took his foot off the accelerator, used the brakes gently, and brought it under control.

"What now, Skip?" he asked. "She won't steer worth a damn."

"Oughta be a garage, 'bout four, five miles on," Chappie told him.

"I'll try it," Cotton shrugged. He nursed the old girl along at about ten miles an hour, and we finally made it. The place we pulled into was a typical country garage— cinder yard, one gas pump, lazy dog, a half-dozen beat-up wrecks drowning in a sea of weeds out back. The unpainted, weatherbeaten building looked as if it might have started life as a blacksmith's shop, or maybe a Wells Fargo depot. The faded lettering on a sign across the front said that it was "Owned and Operated by Warren K. Northey."

We filed off the bus, and Chappie went over to confer with the proprietor. In his early fifties, Warren K. Northey was a short, stocky, red-faced man, with the dead stub of a roll-your-own cigarette stuck to his lower lip.

"How long you figure it might take?" Chappie asked him.

The garage man snorted. "How do I know? I ain't even figured a way to get the front end up yet."

"Can't get her on the hoist?"

"Can't even get her inside. Don't fret, though, I'll think of something."

He did, too—about an hour later, after he'd finished changing the oil in a Ford pickup, pumped gas for several cars, and eaten most of his lunch. The solution was to use two jacks, one on either side, which B.G. and Woodrow Wilson Jones worked in tandem while Warren K. supervised the operation.

"Ol' gal look lak she gettin' ready to take a shit," Latimore Lee said, as she sat back on her rear tires.

"Ah'd shit if I had to go in there," Sweetcorn said, as Northey squirmed under the front end on his back.

"Axel," he said, when he crawled out five minutes later. "Cracked just about right through."

"What can we do 'bout that?" Chappie asked.

Northey took off his cap and used it to wipe the sweat from his forehead. There were little clusters of cinders stuck to the grease on the back of his faded coveralls.

"Well, we can send into Superior for a new one. Oughta get here tomorrow, if they got one in stock; run you maybe twenty-five bucks. Or I can weld the son-of-a-buck for ten."

"The weld hold up?" Chappie wanted to know.

"Stronger than before," Northey said. "Like when they set a broken bone."

"How long that take?" Chappie asked.

"Oh, an hour and a half, maybe two."

"Better weld her then," Chappie said.

"All right."

"Seems I 'member a place to eat not far off," Chappie said.

"Sure, Fran's place. You can walk it easy."

"Think they'll serve us there?" Chappie asked.

Northey laughed. "Fran'd serve the devil himself if she figured he could pay."

"You're in, B.G.," Malachi said.

They started off, straggling along in clusters of two and three. At the edge of the highway, Buck turned and looked back.

"You comin'?" he asked.

Hoping to see Mary Lou before the game, I had taken off the lampblack when I shaved that morning.

"I'm not hungry," I told him.

"Suit yo'self," he said.

Left alone, I didn't know what to do with myself. The sun was hot in the empty sky, and there wasn't any shade. Nowhere to sit, nothing to read. Every few minutes the garageman had to crawl out from under the front end to service the gas pump. Three or four times he stopped to roll a cigarette, taking a couple of deep drags each time, then letting the fire go out. I think he just liked making them. Another hour drifted by, and he still didn't even have the wheels off. At that rate, I thought, we would be there until Christmas.

"You mind if I use your phone?" I asked him. Information could no doubt give me Mary Lou's home number. "It'll be long distance, but I'll pay the charges."

His voice from under the bus was muffled, and I had to lean down to hear him.

"Wouldn't mind, if I had one," he said.

"No phone?"

"Had her taken out two years ago," he said. "Ain't never missed it."

Oh, that's just great, I thought. That's fine.

He stuck his head out.

"Mind if I ask you a question?"

"Shoot," I said.

"Them ballplayers, they're all niggers."

"That isn't a question," I told him.

"Well, here's one—what are you doin' with them?"

"I own them."

153

He nodded, satisfied. "Sure," he said, "I shoulda been able to figure that out."

"I got one for you," I said.

"What's that?"

"When are you gonna have that axel fixed?"

"I'm doin' the best I can," he said. "Won't take long, once I get her off."

"Then let's get her off."

"Sure. I just didn't know where you fit, that's all."

Soon after that the others came drifting back, a few at a time. Buck brought me a couple of hot dogs, wrapped in wax paper, and a lukewarm bottle of Coca-Cola.

"Starvin' won't help," he said.

"Won't help what?" I asked him.

"Get us to Hobblin," he said, looking me right in the eye.

"Thanks, Buck," I said.

"Just pay me," he said. "I ever tell you 'bout the little fox I had in Fort Wayne, Indiana?"

"Yeah, you did."

Buck nodded. "Figured I must have," he said.

The afternoon dragged on. The All Stars stood around, talked, joked, scuffed at the cinders with their feet. B.G. found a couple of square yards of shade at the side of the garage, and fell asleep. Malachi started up the travelling poker game, but it broke up after a little while because the sun was too naked and glaring on the cards. Some of the others played a game flipping Sweetcorn's big pocket knife until they got bored with it. Later five or six went across the road to play pepper on some bumpy pasture land, which had been grazed over by dairy cows that had moved away a short distance and

154

stood listlessly, chewing grass; baseball, in some form or another, was always the secure, familiar, ultimate resort.

Meanwhile, Warren K. Northey plodded along in his lethargic, disjointed fashion. Cars kept coming in for gas and the proprietor didn't let one get away without sharing some relaxed conversation with its owner; the weather, the crop outlook, and the latest exploits of Fibber McGee and Molly on radio were each discussed three or four times. Every fifteen minutes or so he would take the makings from his coveralls' pocket and build another smoke, a ritual he performed with exasperating patience. He must have had the world's weakest kidneys. And, when he was working, he spent most of his time looking for misplaced tools and parts.

I got so mad that I was tempted to kick the jacks out while he was under the chassis.

"Look," I suggested at one point, "why don't I take care of the pumps, and you stay on the job?"

"That's right decent," he said, "but why not get one of your niggers to do it?"

"They don't know how to make change," I said.

"No, I don't guess so," he said. "Well, I'm obliged."

Eventually he got the axel out and carried it into the garage. Then, for what seemed like an eternity, the shadowy gloom in there was lit up by the blue, white and orange flame of his welding torch. Jesus, I thought after a while, you could patch up the *Titanic* in less time.

Next, there was a long sequence during which Warren K. crawled back underneath again and tried to put the whole thing back together. Maybe because he wasn't too sure it would all work out, his kidneys seemed to give him particular trouble at that stage.

155

But at long last he emerged for the final time.

"That oughta do it," he said, reaching for his tobacco and papers. "You can let her down now."

A couple of the others started to slack off the jacks, while I followed Warren K. and Chappie into the garage.

"How much it come to?" Chappie asked.

"Hold your horses 'till I figure it," the garageman told him. He found the stub of a pencil, and wrote down a figure, then a second underneath it. I don't know whether he was trying to add or multiply, but whatever it was didn't work out.

"Oh, hell," he said, "make it fifteen bucks."

Chappie took a thin roll of bills from his pocket and peeled off a ten, and then a five.

"Much obliged," he said, turning away. He was as anxious as I was to get to Hobblin, although he only had one reason.

Warren K. stared at me. "How come you let him handle the money?" he asked.

"Oh, he's my smart nigger," I said, as I turned away and hurried after Chappie.

By then the sun was beginning to get low in the sky and we still had a lot of miles to make. Buck, back at the wheel at last, poured on the coal until Gabriel shimmied and shook, but it was after six o'clock when we hit Superior, Wisconsin. We curled around the end of Lake Superior, past grain elevators, ships and loading docks, then crossed a long swing bridge into Duluth, Minnesota. There, Buck had to curse and sweet talk the old girl up one of the steepest hills I ever saw, a brute that climbed almost straight up from the waterfront, before we at last turned onto the highway that would take us to Hobblin.

156

About that point Chappie began to relax some with the realization that we should make it in time for the game, although probably not with much to spare. But my secret hope, bloodied and bruised by the kicking around it had taken all day, was sinking fast.

It went to its reward about 7:26 that evening, after interminable miles of peering ahead, desperately looking for some indication that we were approaching our destination. By the time I finally saw the first highway sign that said HOBBLIN, I was sure that we had gone clear across the state of Minnesota and out the other side.

And it was too late.

"All right, let's get changed," Chappie said, standing up in the aisle and looking back along the bus. "Gonna have to move it."

So, scratch Plan 'A.'

We restled around in our seats, pulling on our uniforms. I was applying the familiar lampblack when Buck pulled Gabriel off the highway and headed toward the ball park. There were houses, some already with lights in their windows, on either side of the exit ramp.

I felt panicky, trapped.

Well, I'd find some way to see Mary Lou after the game—even if that meant cutting a hog on Chappie.

I didn't like the idea a whole lot, but I knew that I'd do it, if there was no other way.

Just that one time.

# XIII

We had to cut shadow ball a little short, but we were ready to go by the eight o'clock starting time. It was a nice little park, and the stands were nearly full as Pete Simpson got ready to lead off for us.

A high school marching band had played the national anthem, and the plate umpire turned, his mask in one hand at his hip, to announce the starting batteries:

"For the All Stars, Lee will pitch, Pickett catch. For the home team, Clyde Everett on the mound, Tom Foley behind the plate. Play ball!"

Everett? That would have to be Mary Lou's brother, or perhaps her cousin. Out on the mound a tall, good-looking, young right-hander was taking his warm-up throws. I had seen him before, that first night in the bowling alley. The same "Clyde" who had felt obligated to protect her.

I didn't have time to think about that much before Pete stepped into the batter's box. The first pitch was a blazing fastball—about a foot inside and a foot high. A knock-downer. Pete leaned out of there, propping himself up with his bat to keep from falling backwards into the dirt.

There was a cheer from the fans.

"Oh, hell," Buck said, beside me, "not one of those!"

"Wild as a red-tailed hawk," Cotton added, shaking his head.

The second pitch was also high and tight. Twisting to get away from it, Pete half swung in self-defense. The ball trickled off his bat and rolled to the third baseman, who threw him out by a step or two.

The crowd clapped and shouted its approval.

Buck, our next hitter, was knocked down twice, then took a third fastball in the side, just under his rib cage. Face contorted with pain, he slumped to his knees as if he had been shot. Chappie went out to him, and a minute or so later Buck got to his feet and trotted down to first, his teeth still clenched and his legs rubbery.

The fans seemed to like that too.

"Way to go, Clyde, baby!"

"Keep pourin' it in there!"

"Tell 'em who you are!"

It was the one thing we feared most—a local hotshot with a swelled head who was fired up to challenge us. That route led to Uglysville, U.S.A.

"Don't get riled up none," Chappie said, walking along the front of the dugout. "Just do what you gotta do and let's get out of here."

"Hell, that fucker's low-bridgin' us, Mr. Johnson," Woodrow Wilson Jones said.

"Yeah, well, keep duckin'," Chappie told him.

Malachi managed to twist around enough on another

159

inside fastball to drop a perfect sacrifice bunt down the first base line, advancing Buck to second.

Cotton, batting cleanup, dug in at the plate. Still head-hunting, Clyde Everett brushed him back twice, but his third pitch was not quite as fast and came in over the inside corner. Cotton leaned back a little and hit it about a mile and a half over the left field fence.

All Stars 2, Home Team 0.

B.G. was due up next.

"Get out," Chappie told him, as Buck and Cotton headed in after rounding the bases.

"Aw, shit," Meat said, "I can pound on this fucker. He ain't gonna knock me down."

"We got all we need for now," Chappie said. "Just make it look good, you hear?"

B.G. did as he'd been told, flailing away at three fast balls that were in around his chin. Strike one. Strike two. Strike three, to end the inning. The fans, thinking that their hero had really done it, applauded wildly.

"Aw, shit," B.G. muttered as he waddled in to put on the pads.

"The son of a bitch is gonna stick it in somebody's ear," Cotton said, as we trotted out onto the field.

The crowd was still buzzing, and seemed to be worked up almost into a frenzy. I was aware of that sea of excited faces behind me as I tossed grounders to Malachi, Sweetcorn and Cotton. It was frightening, and all we had done was show up and try to keep from getting our heads knocked off.

Latimore got their leadoff man with a curve that broke in from somewhere in Kansas. The next hitter took two fast balls that he never saw, then waved desperately at a third. The ball came off the handle and arched lazily up into foul territory on the first base side. I drifted over near the stands to gather in the pop-up—as automatic an out as you'd ever hope to see.

Close up the noise of the crowd sounded different, and I realized that most of it was being made by a loud and volatile minority. That made sense: there was no reason why the fans in Hobblin should be much different from any others.

I cushioned the ball in my glove, then glanced up. There was a group of fifteen or twenty right above me, clustered behind the front row railing. They were acting like animals—shouting, screaming, waving clenched fists in the air, each trying to be louder and more insulting than the next, all wanting to start something. They were young, around my age, and about half of them were girls. Nice looking, clean cut, well-dressed young people —with hatred in their eyes and on their faces.

And, in the middle of the group, jumping up and down, blonde hair tossing from side to side, was Mary Lou Everett.

She was looking right at me, and her mouth opened wide—the mouth I had so much wanted to kiss again.

"Drop it, you spade nigger!"

I stared at her, stunned, unable to believe that so pretty a face could ever be so primally ugly, so distorted, so obscene. I was glad then for the lampblack mask.

Other shouts and insults poured down over me.

"Clyde'll get ya, ya black bastard!"

"Your turn's comin', nigger boy!"

"It's open season on 'coons!"

But none of that mattered any longer. I just stood

161

there for what seemed like a very long time. Then I heard Cotton's voice, penetrating the cacophony above me.

"C'mon, baby. Attaboy. Hey, hey, let's go."

Reacting instinctively, I turned back toward the diamond and fired the ball to him. There was a little reassurance in that, and I struggled desperately to wipe away the shock by concentrating on the ball game, on what was familiar and normal. But I don't remember how we got their third batter out to end the inning.

There was a lot of tension in the dugout because we all knew that something was building up, and we were apprehensive about how it might end. Chappie, his eyes darting this way and that, strolled back and forth in front of us.

"Keep it cool," he kept saying, half under his breath. "Keep it cool."

Clyde Everett was still throwing at us. Woodrow Wilson Jones had to hit the dirt twice before he managed to lean back and fly out to deep center. Every pitch was vicious. Sweetcorn did his best to turn it into comedy. Dancing out to the plate, he lay down on his stomach in the batter's box.

"I'se ready! I'se ready!" he screeched, glancing back over his shoulder at the crowd. Then he got up, and ran around to hide behind the plate umpire. It was a brilliant try, and many of the fans laughed; but things had already gone too far by then to be denied some kind of climax.

I was the next batter. The first two pitches were inside and high, and I had to suck my chest in tight to my backbone to keep from getting cut down. Then Clyde threw three fastballs over the outside corner, I could have ripped any one of them for extra bases, but all I wanted to do was to get it over with as quickly as possible. The umpire called me out on strikes, and there was another jubilant outburst from Mary Lou and her friends.

Latimore cut them down on eleven pitches in their half of the second—it would have been nine except that the ump guessed wrong on two hummers he never saw. There was nothing fancy about it; The Eggman just reared back and overpowered the hitters.

I began to think it might be all right after all. To every intent and purpose the game had ceased to be an exhibition contest—hardly any reams or funny stuff, just three up and three down. We wouldn't need any more runs, and we wouldn't let them have any. Just hope that nobody got killed by crazy Clyde Everett—the other Everett—and it would be over in another hour or so.

It didn't work out exactly like that.

Before we took the field again, Chappie spoke with Latimore.

"Keep it movin' fast as you can," he said, "only don't strike 'em all out. Them people riled up too much already, you understand?"

"I know, I know," Latimore said.

"Grounders and fly balls is just as quick," Chappie said.

I kept my eyes away from the stands because I didn't want to see Mary Lou again. The noise grew even louder and more feverish behind me, but I never did have rabbits' ears and managed to shut most of it out.

Latimore struck out the first batter with some more smoke, then eased up on the next hitter, who got enough

163

wood on the ball to laft a dinky little fly to Woodrow Wilson Jones. Then Clyde Everett stepped into the batter's box, and the shouting and yelling reached new heights.

Latimore fed him one real fastball, just to let him know who was boss, then eased off on the next pitch. Everett chopped it to Sweetcorn on three nice, high bounces. I watched the graceful arc of the throw, relaxed in the assurance that we had the runner by a good eight or ten feet. Suddenly I saw something out of the corner of my eye that I just couldn't believe: *the crazy son of a bitch was sliding into first base!*

Caught so completely by surprise, I didn't have time to react before the spikes drove into my leg just above the knee and I went sprawling and rolling in the dirt. Somehow I held onto the ball, but I wasn't thinking about that then. The whole area around my knee felt like it was on fire. When I sat up I saw blood oozing out in three or four places where the spikes had driven through the heavy uniform cloth.

Clyde Everett came back, brushing himself off, and looked down at me.

"How do you like it, nigger?"

I wanted to get up and kill him, but then Chappie was kneeling beside me. Cotton, Malachi, Buck and the others were there too, in a closing, protective circle. Beyond them I could hear some of the fans screaming and jeering.

"Aw-right, take it easy now," Chappie was saying. "Least you still got your cap on."

"Yeah, I don't know about my leg, though."

"Bad?"

164

Actually the pain was beginning to ease some; the knee was throbbing like hell where the blunt spikes had ripped into the flesh, but I didn't think there was anything broken or torn inside.

"It's coming," I said.

"You knows I can't look at it out here."

Oh, shit, I thought, the damned white skin again.

"I know," I said. "It'll keep."

"This oughta do for now," he said, taking a big bottle of iodine from his windbreaker pocket. He poured some of the brown liquid through and around the jagged tears in my pants. It stung like the hammers of hell.

"You walk?" Chappie asked.

I got up, hobbled a couple of steps, then started to trot gingerly toward the dugout. The All Stars formed a kind of a convoy, some in front, some in back of me. With the blood and the iodine stains, the knee was a mess to look at, but it held up under my weight.

"It's all right," I told Chappie.

"That's good," he said.

Mary Lou Everett and the rest of her zoo behind first base were whooping it up, enjoying themselves, but quite a few of the other fans clapped politely for me.

"Luke can finish up at first," Chappie said, as we got to the bench.

"Like hell," I told him. They weren't going to get that satisfaction.

Chappie looked at me for a minute, then nodded.

"Suit yo'self," he said.

The innings went by quickly—the fifth, sixth, seventh, eighth. Latimore remained in complete control, letting some batters pop-up or ground out, blazing his fastball past others to remind them who was boss. On their side, Clyde Everett continued to throw at us, pitch after pitch. B.G. was hit on the fat of his upper arm, and Woodrow Wilson Jones in the small of the back. We could have just ducked and taken one walk after another, but that would only have inflamed the lunatic segment still further. Instead, wanting to avoid any further incidents, we squirmed and danced in the batters' box, trying not to get killed while doing our best to get out by blooping flyballs and squibbing grounders that even those country boys could handle. Clyde Everett was just a wild, crazy thrower, who would never learn to be a pitcher, if he lived to be a thousand.

It came down, finally, to the last of the ninth; score still All Stars 2, Home Team 0. Just three more outs, then farewell to Hobblin, Minnesota. Anxious to finish it off, Latimore got two of them on six straight fast balls. I doubt that Ty Cobb could have fouled off even one of them. Then Clyde Everett sauntered to the plate, accompanied by a defiant, last ditch chorus from Mary Lou and her friends.

Latimore bore down still harder. The batter took the first pitch, which he never saw, then flailed blindly at the second. By pure luck the bat made contact, and the ball was lined out of the infield, tailing away into the right field corner. Woodrow Wilson Jones played the carom off the fence perfectly and fired the ball into second on one bounce. A stand-up double all the way—and the first hit of the game off Latimore.

But Clyde Everett wasn't satisfied with that. Sweetcorn was about six feet past second base, on the left field side, when he took the throw from Woodrow Wilson

Jones. Everett went barreling right past the bag and drove into him like a pulling guard blocking out a linebacker. Sweetcorn, as thin and vulnerable as a long strand of dry spaghetti, just kind of flew apart, the ball rolling loose. Pete Simpson, backing up the play, retrieved it and snapped a throw to second. Scurrying back, the runner slid in safely, his spikes again flashing high. Cotton came out of it with blood running down his bare right arm, and dripping from the tips of his fingers. He turned to the base umpire and called time, then jogged in toward the mound. Malachi, B.G. and I converged to meet him there. Behind me, the zoo was going crazy. The thought crossed my mind that we could still lose the damn ball game.

It was Cotton's court. He held the ball in his right hand, and there were blood stains on it. Sweetcorn was on his feet at the back of the base path, bent over, knees still weak, trying to get some air back into his lungs.

"That is all there is gonna be of this bull shit," Cotton said.

"You right, Cotton," Malachi told him, "enough is enough."

"What's you thinkin'?" B.G. asked.

Cotton looked at Latimore.

"You know, don't you?"

"I knows," the pitcher said. "First pitch?"

"Yeah," Cotton told him.

"Let's do it then."

The conference over, I ran back to first, not knowing what was going to happen.

The plate umpire called time in. Cocky, with his cheering section loud in its encouragement, Clyde Everett took a long lead off second—a stupid lead with his team a couple of runs behind and two out in the ninth.

On the mound, Latimore turned the ball around and around in his long fingers as he peered in at the plate. The Eggman had the best pick-off motion I ever saw. He took his exaggerated wind-up, came to the set position, then whirled quickly and fired the ball to second base, where Cotton had moved in behind the runner.

Clyde Everett was caught about eight feet off the bag, with no chance of getting back. In desperation, he turned away and dug in for third. Sweetcorn was still crouched over, trying to recover. Latimore went over to back up Malachi, and I ran across to cover second, but neither of us played any part in the subsequent rundown —that was enacted entirely by Cotton, Malachi and the monkey-in-the-middle base runner.

Terrified, but still resourceful, he was a frightened animal, taking a few steps in one direction, then putting on the brakes and trying to scramble back in the other. Cotton and Malachi kept shortening the distance, moving in for the kill. The ball went back and forth between them, each throw like a rifle shot, an assassin's bullet, none more than two or three inches away from their quarry's head. It was a deadly game, and I almost felt sorry for Clyde Everett—almost but not quite. There was panic in his eyes and in the slack jawed, open-mouthed expression on his face. I'd seen that same look once on a marten with its leg caught in a spring trap.

Malachi to Cotton . . . Cotton to Malachi . . . closer and closer. Clyde Everett was running out of room. Finally, unable to stand it any longer, he dove to one side, and curled up at the edge of the base path, like a small child asleep in a dark room.

Cotton looked down at him with contempt for a moment, then went over and, almost gently, tagged him with the ball. Off to one side, the base umpire jerked his thumb up in the air. Out! The game was over.

This tense sequence had been acted out in almost total silence. Most of the fans had just sat there, stunned, and even the Clyde Everett cheering section had suspended operations. As soon as it was played out, though, there was a renewed buzz of hostility behind me. I glanced over, and Mary Lou's friends were dropping down from the first base stands and coming across the diamond after us.

Then I heard Chappie's voice. He was standing on the grass just beyond third base, yelling at us and gesturing that we should follow him. I ran in that direction as hard as I could go, joining up with Buck and Woodrow Wilson Jones as we crossed the left field foul line and sprinted for the exit in the fence.

The bus and truck were parked just outside, with their motors running. Luke Redding, the other pitcher, was at the wheel of the truck and Chappie was driving the bus. It was like Chappie, I thought, to figure out what was likely to happen and have them there waiting for us.

We scrambled on board, me last, and Chappie swung the door closed behind us, throwing the motor into gear at the same time.

By then the first of our pursuers was coming through the gate.

"Let's get outa here," B.G. said.

" 'Bout what I had in mind," Chappie said, pushing down on the gas pedal.

169

# XIV

We got out of town and turned onto a secondary highway. Woodrow Wilson Jones had taken over the wheel
as soon as we were clear of the outskirts. The truck was
following along as usual, about a hundred yards back.

"What you want to do, Mr. Johnson?" Woodrow
asked.

" 'Bout what?"

" 'Bout the lights," Woodrow said.

That problem hadn't crossed my mind until then.

"Right now, we gonna eat," Chappie told him. "Ought
to be a place 'bout fifteen minutes along here."

"Uh-huh."

"Give 'em a spell to cool out," Chappie said.

"We'll go back in after?" Buck asked.

"Well, we ain't gonna leave them there," Chappie told
him.

"No, I guess not."

So we weren't quite finished with Hobblin after all.

Chappie turned and looked back.

"Now 'bout tonight," he said, "Mr. Malachi and Mr. Cotton, you is both fined one week's pay. So is you, Mr. Latimore Lee."

"What?"

"That don't strike me as fair."

"He was askin' for it all night."

Chappie nodded. "Doin' that, sure enough," he acknowledged.

"Then how come you finin' us?"

Chappie sighed. " 'Cause we won't be able to come in here no more, and this town's always been a good date."

"Who needs the damn place?" Malachi asked.

"We do," Chappie told him, "if we ever gets the lights back, that is."

"Well, it was worth it," Cotton said.

"Oh, yeah," Malachi said, laughing, "it was."

Latimore giggled. "We really got all of him, didn't we?" he asked.

"Every little piece," Chappie said, his face breaking into a grin, "but you is still fined."

"Mr. Johnson," Woodrow broke in.

"Yeah."

"They is a couple of cars behind us," Woodrow said, glancing up at the rear view mirror.

"What about it?" Chappie asked. "This here's a road, ain't it?"

"They is comin' up awful fast," Woodrow replied.

We all turned and looked out through the back windows. There were two pairs of headlights, and just then one set swung wide as the driver pulled out to pass the truck. The second car followed, hard on its heels. The small circles of brilliant light swayed erratically from

171

side to side, and the beams tilted up and down against the blackness as the front wheels bounced over the uneven blacktop surface.

Oh, they were coming, all right.

"Let 'em go on by," Chappie said to Woodrow.

"I will, if they will," Woodrow said.

But that wasn't what they had in mind. A minute or so later the lead car caught up to us and stayed alongside, careening wildly. There were eight or nine young people jammed into the front and back seats. The windows were rolled down, and they were leaning out, screaming, laughing, jeering up at us. I caught a glimpse of Mary Lou's face.

Crazy wild. Crazy reckless. Crazy.

The driver of the big Buick kept swerving in toward our front wheels, the way a wolf snaps at and worries a doe in deep snow. Woodrow eased the bus over until the outside wheels were away over on the shoulder, and there was no more room—nothing beyond except fence posts and trees and boulders. Shattering glass and crumpling metal.

After a mile or so the first car dropped back, and let the second move in for its share of fun and games. The harassment went on without letup—the squeal of brakes, the protest of tormented rubber, sparks shooting out, the clang of steel on steel as car and bus came together and glanced apart.

They kept coming on in relays. Mile after mile went by, and the place where we were supposed to eat was long gone behind us.

Woodrow was good, and he kept his cool, tightroping along the brink of the ditch, steering us out of one jam

172

after another. A couple of times he managed to nose the bus out in front of the lead car, then zig-zagged to keep it cut off behind us. We went over more than one hill in the wrong lane, praying that we wouldn't meet head-on with some farmer and his wife coming home from a euchre party.

The odds, though, were all with the cars; Gabriel did her best to jive, but she was too old, didn't have the speed, and was about as easy to maneuver as a cement bridge.

I knew that it couldn't go on much longer; sooner or later people were going to get killed, some of us, or some of them, or maybe some of both.

Inside the bus it was wild. Loose bits of gear were rattling and clanging everywhere. We sat with our feet and backs braced to keep from getting thrown into the aisle.

"I gonna turn off, first chance I get," Woodrow shouted back at us.

Apparently, nobody could come up with a better idea, and we had to try something. We went another mile or so, and then the bouncing headlights picked up a small sign saying that we were coming up on County Road 33.

"Grab somethin'," Woodrow yelled over his shoulder, "'cause here we go!"

He waited until we were almost on top of the intersection before he started to pump the brakes, gently at first, then more and more urgently. We were still going too fast when we hit the loose gravel, and went into a lurching, sideways skid. The headlights swung around, and I saw tree trunks looming up in the window across from me.

Woodrow fought the wheel, and used the gas and brake pedals like a pump organist playing "The Flight of the Bumblebee." It was touch-and-go, but somehow he and old Gabriel pulled us out of it. Suddenly, miraculously, the bus was going along a narrow, dirt road, still basically a runaway, but coming gradually under control.

"Aw, shit!" Woodrow said, almost to himself.

I couldn't see it from where I sat, but the road just ahead was covered with water, only an inch or two, but enough to turn the surface into slick, toboggan slide gumbo. The work of beavers, probably. Anyway, too close to do anything about it. We hit the water, and were skidding again, this time still more violently. Gabriel went around two or three times, like a merry-go-round gone berserk, and finally came to a stop, still on the road, but facing back the way we had come.

There was no time to feel relief, because just then the two cars turned in after us. Momentarily taken by surprise, they had overshot the intersection, but now they were back. They pulled up, side by side, maybe fifty feet away. Luke swung the truck in from the highway and stopped behind them.

So there we all were. After the crazy chase, it seemed strange to be standing still, the sudden silence of the black night all around us. A cloud of dust drifted across our headlights, and there was just the "mar-oom, mar-oom" of a bullfrog from nearby in the swamp.

For long seconds nobody seemed to know what to do. It was Buck who finally took command.

"Come on, let's go," he shouted. "Everybody take one." He was standing next to Woodrow, beside the

174

front door, holding open the canvas bat bag, from which a dozen or so taped handles protruded.

We hesitated.

"What you plannin'?" Chappie asked him.

"We go after them," Buck said, "or they come after us. Let's make it our way."

"I guess yo' right," Chappie said, starting for the door. We followed him, each pulling out a bat before stepping down into the night. Everybody automatically selected his own favorite model—mine a black Louisville Slugger with a long, thin handle.

Buck was the last one out. Brandishing our bats, we moved toward the cars, in a ragged line that spread across the country road, B.G. led the way. With the headlights of the bus behind him, he must have looked even bigger and more menacing than life. We moved deliberately, not hurrying. Apart from our shuffling feet, the bullfrog still had a monopoly on the sound effects.

The cars just sat there as we advanced slowly toward them, and we had covered about half the ground before we heard voices. Then there was a babble of excitement.

"Let's get us some niggers!"

"Right!"

"Split some heads!"

"Right!"

"Stomp on 'em!"

"Yeah!"

"Lynch 'em! String 'em up!"

"Right!"

We kept advancing.

The front doors of the cars flew open and a half-dozen figures emerged, shadowy in the dim headlights. There

175

are probably a few more of them, I thought, than there are of us, if you count Mary Lou and the other girls.

Maybe thirty feet to go. My fingers tightened around the bat handle. Then the tone of the voices changed abruptly.

"We taught 'em a lesson, right?"

"Oh, yeah!"

"They know they ain't welcome, right?"

"Black bastards!"

"Come on—we've wasted enough time."

"Yeah, let's go."

"Right!"

We were almost on top of them by then, near enough to make out individual faces, ghostly white but blotched with shadows.

"Get in here, Pudge!" a voice hollered.

"Move, for Christ's sake!"

Pudge and his friends scurried back inside, scrambling and elbowing in their sudden haste. Car doors slammed behind them. The motors roared into life.

Simultaneously, the cars leaped backwards, tires clawing at the gravel, front wheels cut as sharply as they would go. They jerked to a stop just short of the ditch, then leaped ahead together. There wasn't much room on the narrow road, but both drivers made it by the skin of their teeth, bringing the swerving, skidding cars around just short of the trees on the opposite side, and steering them back toward the highway. Suddenly we were looking at red taillights.

Luke pulled the truck over to the side to let them pass. They went up the grade to the intersection, and turned left toward town. We could hear the roar of their accelerating motors for a moment, and then they were gone.

We stood where we were, still more or less in line, the bats hanging loosely from our hands.

"Guess that's it," Cotton said.

It was over, but there was no sense of elation, or of winning; we had come out of it, saved our skins, survived —that was all.

"Let's go eat," Chappie said.

A couple of hours later we found our way back to the town, and, in it, the ball park. There were no lights in the windows of the houses by then, and the streets were deserted.

A half-moon was shining, which made it a little easier to take down the lights and load the truck. The only visitor we had was a small mongrel dog that attached itself to Chappie.

Dawn couldn't have been far away when we finally hit the road.

So long, Hobblin.

Good-bye, Mary Lou.

# XV

The days of August fell away, joining those of July in the file of that summer. For the All Stars they were recorded only in the box scores that appeared in the small town newspapers of the American and Canadian mid-west—the Lethbridge *Herald,* the *Twin Lakes Times-Expositor,* the Souris *Plain Dealer.*

We went back up into Canada again for a couple of weeks, crossing Manitoba and part of Saskatchewan, playing places like Pilot Mound, Carman, Minnedosa and Weyburn.

We won every game, as we were expected to do, and almost all by two runs: 4–2, 6–4, 3–1. That was the margin Chappie liked best. He was dead set against running up the score because "rubbin' it in gets people's blood angry." On the other hand, one-run leads made him uneasy.

"Never can tell in this game," he said. "Now say we got one run on them, and they comin' up in the ninth. 'Spose they puts a runner on some way. Then 'spose

178

somebody gets lucky 'n hits one out. It can happen. Ain't just that we lose, but maybe other teams start thinkin' they can beat us. And then it ain't so nice any more."

We tried never to shut the home team out; this happened only that one time, in Hobblin.

The days were growing noticeably shorter. When I first joined the club we used to play two, maybe even three, innings in lingering daylight, but by the middle of August the lights were usually on by the time the ump hollered "Play ball!" to start the game.

The grasshoppers came, not in a plague, but enough to ripple the grass and weeds in front of you as you walked along.

The sweet corn ripened, and you could buy all you wanted from the farmers for next to nothing. One day Chappie got six dozen cobs for a buck and a half. We found an old wash tub to cook it in, and had a feast beside a river near Carman, Manitoba. There was plenty of butter, and I guess Chappie contributed that too.

The wheat was turning to burnished gold as it headed out, and it still looked good.

About the middle of the month we pulled in to a town called Bensford. It was early evening of a day that had been almost unbearably hot, ominously still, with hardly a breath of air.

There was a strange, yellowish color to the western sky as we set up the lights. Chappie kept watching the low-hanging clouds, as they formed and reformed. The atmosphere was somehow unnatural, menacing.

But a good crowd showed up, and the fans stayed, in spite of a thunderstorm that broke just as we were finishing shadow ball. It rained hard, and there was some wicked lightning, but it didn't last long and we were able to get the game underway about twenty minutes late.

The rain did nothing to clear the air. Neither did another short downpour that held up play again as we were getting ready to bat in the seventh. Chappie was a little more relaxed by then, because we had got in enough innings to make it a legal contest and ensure our share of the gate receipts. But it was still just as hot, just as oppressive, just as foreboding. The clouds continued to roll by, just beyond the range of the lights, and it was as if we were playing in a big, airless tent that was about ready to collapse.

"Let's get it over," Chappie said, and nobody was disposed to argue with him.

We hustled through the remaining innings, making it look as if we were doing our best to increase our 4–2 lead, while having a hard time preserving it. Luke Redding, on the mound for us, set up their last batter with a rinkydink curve, then struck him out with two blue darter fastballs to end the game.

Because of the delays, it was late by then, getting on toward midnight. The fans drifted away quickly out of the stands. That same weird, yellow light was back in the sky as we strung out along the foul lines to start taking down the equipment. I don't know what caused it; there was no moon that night.

"Gotta hustle, gotta hustle," Chappie yelled, as he trotted out to take charge of the operation—something he had never done before.

We were about half way through when the twister struck. The first thing I knew about it was when I heard Cotton's exclamation.

180

"Jesus, what the hell is that?"

I could see him quite clearly in the unreal light, and I turned my head to follow his stare. There was a black funnel, the color of death, bearing down on us from out of that yellow sky. It was the most terrifying thing I had ever seen, a swirling, evil coil of ten thousand snakes. Writhing, seething, angry, utterly malevolent. Scarcely moving, yet closing in at incredible speed.

The wind came first. There was no gradual build-up; after those hushed, breathless hours, it was just suddenly there, a terrible force pledged to the destruction of everything in its path. I staggered back, all the air sucked out of my lungs.

Then the rain, driving at us horizontally in solid sheets, dense enough to drown you standing up, blotting out the world.

In the final instant I saw a silhouetted figure, sprawling grotesquely, as it tumbled down from the top of the right field light standard. God, I thought, that's Malachi, and he must be hurt. Badly hurt.

Hammered to my hands and knees, I sprawled flat against the earth, fingers clawing and toes groping desperately for some hold that would save me from being blown away.

I clung there for what seemed like a month. The hellish wind rose to a final frenzy before passing on to terrorize, and perhaps kill, some other people. Simultaneously, the rain slackened and petered out.

It was over. There was just the empty, brooding silence. A sudden chill in the air. An enormous sense of relief.

I lay there for another thirty seconds, then staggered

up on wobbly legs. It was pitch black, but I sensed movement nearby. Chappie's gravelly voice came through the darkness.

"B.G., you there?"

"Yeah, yeah."

"Buck?"

"Uh-huh."

"Joe?"

"I'm all right," I called out.

"Malachi?"

No answer.

"Buck, Joe, see to him," Chappie told us. "Sweetcorn?"

"Sweetcorn's here."

Buck and I went to find Malachi as the roll call continued. When we got to him, Malachi was just coming to. Apparently his left shoulder had absorbed most of the impact when he landed. Then the light standard had come crashing down, knocking him out. As he sat up weakly on the rain-soaked ground, it was obvious that the shoulder was giving him a lot of pain.

"Good thing it's the left one," Buck told him. "You can still throw."

"Sure, sure," Malachi said, "long as somebody there to hand me the ball."

"You think it's busted?" I asked him.

"Ah don' know," he said, through clenched teeth, "Ah never bust it before."

Hampered by the almost total darkness, it was another ten minutes or so before we could add up what the twister had done to us. It might have been a lot worse. Several others had scrapes and bruises, but there were only two real casualties—Malachi, with his bad shoulder, and Woodrow, who had a deep cut just above his right knee.

"Somethin' just come flyin' at me," Woodrow said. "I don' know what it was. Piece of a roof, I think."

Sweetcorn brought the bus in through the main gate, and we got Malachi and Woodrow into it.

"We gonna look for a doctor," Chappie said. "Joe, you come with us. Rest of you see what you can do 'bout the lights."

"Sure."

"Be back as soon as we can," Chappie said as he got on the bus.

Sweetcorn had to ease around a fallen tree near the ball park, and we saw some broken hydro lines that were shooting sparks, but the twister seemed to have just missed the town, leaving it with little damage.

After several blocks we saw a lighted, frosted glass sign that said: "Dr. Wendel Amys, Physician and Surgeon." The big, old red brick house was in darkness as Chappie and I went up the walk, our spikes clattering on the flagstone.

We had to press the button beside the verandah door several times before a light finally went on inside. A few seconds later the door opened, and a tall, raw-boned, elderly man was staring out at us over his glasses. His bald head was fringed with grey, and he was wearing a pair of old fashioned flanelette pajamas and a look that was part puzzled, part wary, and part annoyed. It's probably the first time, I thought, that he's ever been wakened up at one o'clock in the morning by a couple of black ballplayers, half-drowned and still wearing their uniforms.

"What the hell do you want?" he demanded.

"Sorry to get you up," Chappie said, "but they's a couple of my guys hurt on the bus."

"You been in a motor accident?"

Chappie shook his head. "Uh-uh, a twister got us."

"Where? I didn't see any twister."

"Come in 'cross the ball park," Chappie told him. "Could you do somethin' for my players?"

"Well, Christ, I'm up now, anyway," the doctor said. "Let's see what we got."

"Much obliged," Chappie said.

Woodrow hobbled in, with one arm around Sweetcorn's shoulders and the other around mine. Malachi made it on his own, but the pain was clear in his face.

"Like the hammers o' hell," he said.

We must have been there for almost an hour. When it was over Woodrow was sporting about a dozen stitches in his leg, and had been advised to stay off it for at least three or four days.

"I thought he was going to faint on me in there," the doctor said. "First time I ever saw a pale nigger."

I wondered what he would have thought if he had had to sew me up instead of Woodrow.

Malachi's shoulder was strapped with about a mile of adhesive tape. The doctor had given him a hypodermic shot of something to ease the pain, and some pills to take when that began to wear off. He didn't think there was anything torn or broken inside, although the shoulder would be "as sore as a boil for the next while."

"How much'll that be?" Chappie asked when we were all in the outer office again.

"Oh, that's all right," the doctor said. He had pulled a white gown on over his pyjamas, and now it had some of Woodrow's blood on the front of it.

"We wants to pay," Chappie said.

"Well, hell, give me five then."

"Don't seem much for all you done," Chappie told him.

"It's enough."

Chappie took our share of that night's gate receipts out of his hip pocket and handed over a five dollar bill.

"I thank you," Chappie said.

"You don't mind if I go back to bed now?" the doctor asked.

"No, sir," Chappie said, "not at all."

The lights went out inside the house before we reached the bus.

When we returned to the ball park the lighting equipment was stowed away in the truck, and the other players were huddled in the dugout. Somebody had built a fire out of blown-down tree branches and some broken boards from the fence against the chill that had moved in behind the storm front.

Chappie asked about the lights.

"Frames is bent pretty bad here and there," Pete Simpson told him, "probably busted in a coupla places. And we is gonna need a whole mess of new bulbs."

"Get it ready for the game tomorrow?"

"Maybe," Pete shrugged.

Chappie decided that we would spend the night, or what was left of it, where we were. It must have been getting on toward three in the morning by then. We got on the bus, and bedded down under whatever we could find that would help to keep us warm.

Bone weary though I was, I couldn't go to sleep. A lot of thoughts were running around in my mind, especially the realization that the cyclone could just as easily have hit the ball park a half-hour earlier, while the stands were still filled with men, women and children. If that had happened, there would have been a lot of dead and maimed bodies lying around.

Chappie's light was the only one still on in the bus. After twisting and turning for some time, I went up the aisle and dropped into the seat beside him.

"You mind?" I asked him.

"No, I was just sittin' here. It's been a long day."

"And night," I said.

"Yeah."

We talked for a while, about nothing in particular, keeping our voices low so as not to disturb the others. The conversation died away, and I thought he had fallen asleep. Then I heard a faint sound, a kind of moan, almost but not quite muffled. I turned to look at him. His face was an awful grey color, and his mouth was working like that of a fish on the floorboards of a boat, as he tried to get air into his lungs.

"Mr. Johnson," I asked him in alarm, "what's the matter?"

"It ain't nothin'," Chappie gasped. "I'll be all right."

He leaned forward and began to roll his thin chest over the back of the seat in front of us. I was terrified, not knowing what was happening, not knowing what to do. Five minutes went by. Finally, Chappie sank back in the bus seat. His normal color was coming back, and he was breathing easier. Still, he looked like he was about a hundred and four years old.

"Goin' away now," he said.

"Have you had it before?" I asked him.

He nodded. "Oh, yeah."

"What is it?"

"They calls it *angina*, somethin'—I don't know," he said. "Hurts while it lasts, but that ain't long."

"Isn't there anything you can do?"

"Sure they is," he said. "Go sit on a porch somewheres, chasin' the flies off. No more bus, no more shadow, no more nothin'. You see me doin' that?"

"No," I said, "I can't."

"We all gets old," he said. "Ain't like it's gonna kill me. Let's get us some sleep."

He looked almost normal by then, almost like himself.

"Sure," I said, getting up to go back to my seat.

"Oh, one thing, Joe," he said.

"What's that?"

"Might be better if you didn't say nothin'. No sense fussin' them up."

"Don't worry about it," I told him.

"I ain't," Chappie said.

187

# XVI

I woke up the next morning just in time to see the truck drive away, with Buck at the wheel and Chappie in the seat beside him. The angle of the sunlight flooding into the bus told me that it couldn't be any later than about eight o'clock. And already that aging, sick man was setting out to see about getting the lights fixed for the game that night.

Incredible.

My weary eyes and protesting body reminded me that I'd only had about three hours sleep. From the moaning and groaning around me, I knew the others felt just as bad—except for Malachi and Woodrow, who felt worse. For once the Eggman had scratched his pre-dawn foraging expedition, but nobody had enough strength to eat anyway. Not even B.G.

We crawled through that day, hardly speaking and doing nothing that could be left for another time. In the late afternoon Sweetcorn drove us to the next town. Thank God, it was only about thirty miles away.

Like everybody else, I catnapped as much as I could, but I kept thinking about Chappie and wondering how that worn-out body of his could keep going. Remembering what I had seen the night before, I was scared.

He and Buck caught up with us at the ball park about an hour before game time. Buck could hardly stay awake by then. It had been a long day, Buck told us, a day spent waiting around repair shops, arguing, pleading, praying . . . and waiting around some more. At the end of it the light standards had been straightened out and welded back together, the shattered light bulbs had been replaced, and the All Stars were ready for business as usual.

I studied Chappie's face. The lines in it might have been a little more deeply etched, but there were no obvious signs of fatigue, nothing to link back to that terrible pain that had racked his thin chest. No catnaps for him that day, but he was still on his feet, still going strong, still thinking ahead. There was a ball game to be played, that was all.

It was clear by then, though, that we would have to take the field with a patched-up batting order. The All Stars only carried ten players, including the two pitchers, and you needed something like a certificate from the Mayo Clinic to be excused from the starting lineup. But Woodrow's leg caved in under him whenever he tried to stand on it, and Malachi couldn't lift his arm much above his waist. Both of them would be out of action for that night, at least. And that left us two men short.

Chappie called us together. There was a weathered, splintery, bare-wood bench that extended from the stands out along the left field foul line, and we clustered around a section of it.

"Now we is kinda short-handed," he said. "Mr. Latimore Lee will do the pitchin'. Mr. Luke Redding will take care of third base. And I'll be patrollin' right field."

He stopped then, and waited, as if expecting somebody to say something. Nobody did, probably because we all realized that there was no other way; Chappie played, or we forfeited the game—and the gate. Still, it seemed not just wrong to me but somehow indecent. Hell, Chappie would soon be an old man, and his heart was drying up inside him. But I kept quiet, like the others.

"Let's get on with it then," Chappie continued. "I is anxious to see if them lights work."

We started to break up, but then he stopped us.

"Oh, by the way, Mr. Lee," he said, "I'd be obliged if there wasn't too many hit my way."

We all laughed, except Latimore, who nodded, very seriously.

"You got it, Mr. Johnson," he said. "I don't guess they gonna be playin' too much with that part of the field."

"That's good," Chappie told him.

" 'Cept maybe one," Latimore said, "just to keep you honest out there."

"Too late for that," Chappie said. "It better be a little dinky."

He laughed. "Come down right where I is at."

"Won't be hangin' no clothesline," Latimore promised.

"It is, and the next money you sees will be three weeks from tonight," Chappie said.

190

"I look after you," Latimore told him.

He did too, through the first seven innings. Every pitch was inside and tight, and no batter in the history of baseball could have deliberately poked one into right field. Not Ty Cobb. Not Sisler. Not Joe DiMaggio.

Going into the home team's half of the eighth, we had a 3–1 lead, thanks partly to the Texas-league single Chappie had hung over their shortstop with Buck on third. It had been an uneventful ball game. Luke was a better infielder than most, and he played the hot corner that night as if he belonged there. He wanted to try "ain't lookin'," but I turned down the offer.

"Be just like you to throw me a curve ball," I told him.

"Aw, nothin' like that," he said. "I comin' with smoke all the way."

"Thanks, anyway," I told him.

It had given my own heart a twinge or two to see Chappie running out his single, but other than that he hadn't had much to do apart from trotting out to right field and back. Latimore had kept the ball tight to the batters, and there hadn't been anything hit to the right side all night. There hadn't been much hit to the left side either; we were all still very tired and anxious to get in the nine innings.

That was one of the smallest towns on the All Stars' itinerary, and it had the worst ball park we played in that summer. The field wasn't too bad, apart from some rough spots, but the stands and fences looked as if they had been put up back around the time Sherman was advancing on Atlanta, and left to take care of themselves ever since. It had been a long while since that park had heard the clang of a hammer, and it had never known the

191

slap of a paint brush. There were boards missing here and there, and it seemed likely that the next good wind would blow the whole thing down.

The atmosphere of decay and neglect seemed to cast a pall over the fans too, all four or five hundred of them. Our best reams drew only polite applause or scattered laughter. Not hostile, just lethargic.

Latimore got their first batter in the eighth on three consecutive curve balls that left him cross-eyed. Five to go. The next guy, a right-hand hitter, took a slider for a strike, then chopped desperately at a fast ball as he fell out of the batter's box. The ball came off the end of his bat and blooped out toward right field, about twenty feet over my head.

Oh, oh, I thought, there goes Chappie's "little dinky."

He moved over to get under it, a routine fly ball just like ten thousand others he must have caught from Managua, Nicaragua, to Saskatoon, Saskatchewan. The ball had a lot of spin on it, and was fading into foul territory. Chappie read it perfectly, as instinctive a thing as pulling on his windbreaker. But in the last couple of strides his aging body couldn't respond quickly enough to the signals coming from his brain. He almost got it with a desperate lunge, but the ball trickled off the tip of his glove and dropped onto the grass.

Then, from somewhere up in the shadows of the first base stands, came that ripest of all baseball raspberries.

"Go back to the bushes, Johnson!"

Chappie was bent over to pick up the ball when he heard the fan's cry. He straightened up slowly, and there was vast wonderment in his manner. He looked all around that tank town ball park—at the ramshackle wooden stands; at the falling-down fences; at our stuttering, inadequate lighting system; at the peeling scoreboard; at the weedy, prairie grass outfield with its gopher holes.

Then he glanced in the direction of the unseen fan who had heckled him, and shook his head in good-humored amazement.

"How far back can you get?" he asked.

# XVII

On toward the end of August we crossed the border again and swung back down into the States, playing towns in the Dakotas, Minnesota, Iowa and Wisconsin that we had missed on the earlier swing. Chappie said that the All Stars were finished with Canada for that year, and I realized that the ball club's long migration south was starting as the summer began to die behind us. The corn was taller than the strike zone, and the wheat fields stretched, golden and full-headed, as far as you could see. Another ten days, two weeks at the most, and the combines would be rolling—but please, God, don't let there be an early frost. Not after all that waiting.

Malachi and Woodrow recovered from their injuries and got back into the lineup after missing just that one game. They both still hurt some, but not enough for the fans to notice. Chappie was as active and as much in control as ever, and it was tempting to think there had never been that time in the bus when his face had turned the color of wood ashes and his breath had come as if drawn through a wad of cotton batting.

As the summer waned, the danger of war in Europe seemed to ease off a little. Buck and I had come to an informal arrangement so that he bought a newspaper one day, and I the next. We read *The New York Times,* the *Minneapolis Star,* the *Winnipeg Free Press,* the *Chicago Tribune*—whatever we could get. Each day the front pages reported that the international situation remained tense, as one diplomatic crisis followed another. But there was a sameness about the stories, and it was hard to follow the sequence of events, so that one might have read Monday's paper on Friday without realizing that you had lost your place. You became used to it, inured to it, even bored with it. And you didn't notice as what had once seemed unthinkable became possible, then increasingly probable, and, finally, inevitable. It was, I suppose, all part of the conditioning process required before ordinary people from one country will cross borders and oceans to kill ordinary people from another.

Buck didn't think there would be a war, not right away anyway.

"No, they got too much in common, the English and the Germans," he said. "Their rulers—wasn't they cousins or somethin', just a while back? Hitler'll take a little more, all he can get. Then they'll join up, and fight the Russians. That's who they is really scared of, both of them."

"How soon?" I asked.

"Oh, another year," he said, "maybe two or three. They'll go after them one day, though, 'cause it's the common people, doin' it together."

On the 23rd of August we were rained out in Bemidji,

Minnesota. It started pouring down around four in the afternoon, a real cloudburst, and when we got to the ball park the infield was under about six inches of water, and only a beaver could have stole second. Chappie surveyed the dripping, dismal scene for a half-hour or so, and then told us that we could take the night off—as long as we got back to the bus by midnight.

I decided that I wanted to be by myself that evening. It wasn't because I was fed up with being an All Star; I liked the family feeling and the closeness and what we shared. But you could never be alone; the bus was cramped and there was always someone looking over your shoulder. It was important to get away, to escape the claustrophobia. And I needed to indulge myself a little, to spend some money foolishly, to be expansive. To do what *I* wanted to do.

I stripped to the waist, and stepped outside with a bar of soap to let the rain wash away the dirt and the lampblack. Then I shaved in front of the cracked mirror in the back corner of the bus, put on the cleanest clothes I had, and walked uptown.

I bought a *Doc Savage* magazine for a dime at a drug store, and crossed the street to a restaurant called the Silver Moon. It was pleasant inside, and clean, with fresh, white linen on the tables, and two huge fans, with blades like airplane propellors, turning slowly at either end of the high ceiling. An elderly Chinese man smiled as I went in and took me to a table near the back. The place reminded me a lot of the DeLuxe Cafe, back in Trentville. My dad used to meet Harry Theobald, Harold Dormer, and a couple of others from the *Examiner* there almost every night about eight o'clock. They would talk about sports and politics and other things for an hour or so, and then, when he had finished his second cup of coffee, my father would walk the block and a half to the newspaper offices, climb the stairs to the second floor, and write his editorials for the next day. Harry Chung had operated the DeLuxe for longer than I could remember, and over the years my old man had picked up enough Cantonese to say hello and exchange a few words with him about the weather.

The Silver Moon offered a good menu. The full course dinner—roast chicken, hamburg steak and onions, pork chops with apple sauce—was only thirty-five cents, with soup, potatoes, vegetables, dessert and beverage included. Or a hot beef sandwich, with gravy, French fries, and peas, for twenty cents. But I decided to go for the bundle—soup, big sirloin steak with mushrooms, apple pie and ice cream. That would push the bill up close to a buck, but, what the hell, I didn't splurge very often.

There was a radio playing in the kitchen, and the sounds drifted in to me, just loud enough to leave some impressions on my consciousness without interfering with my reading. There was a program of recorded dance music—Raymond Scott's "Toy Trumpet," Artie Shaw's "Deep Purple," and Kay Kyser's version of one of that summer's hits:

> *Three little fishies in an ityy-bitty poo,*
> *Three little fishies and the mama fishie, too,*
> *'Fwim' said the mama fishie,*
> *'Fwim, if you can',*

197

*And they fwam, and they fwam—*
*Right over the dam.*


The fried steak was a little greasy, and Primo Carnera couldn't have cut it with a fork, but it covered most of the plate and tasted just fine.

### RADIO COMMERCIAL
*Call for Phil—lip Mor——riss!*

A couple of teenage girls sat down at a front table and ordered baconburgers and Cokes. Amos 'n Andy came on the radio.

### BROTHER CRAWFORD
I want you to know that my wife is very unhappy.

### AMOS
Well, yeah, I guess she is, at that.

### ANDY
Say, s'cuse me for protrudin', Kingfish, but ain't you got ahold of my watch chain?

### KINGFISH
How do you like that? One of dese solid gold cufflinks of mine musta hooked on dere.

A little later the Chinese waiter brought me my pie and coffee. I was enjoying this rare chance to be alone, the sense of having time to spare, the luxury of a good meal, the reading. The radio continued in the background.

ANNOUNCER

And now stay tuned for this week's visit with—the Goldbergs!

I asked for a second cup of coffee, and turned another page of the magazine. Doc and his friends were in a hell of a jam, and there didn't seem to be any way out of it.

MOLLY GOLDBERG

Better a crust of bread and enjoy it, than a cake that gives you indigestion.

Then a new voice came on the air, and the abrupt transition commanded my full attention.

ANNOUNCER

We interrupt this program to bring you a special CBS news bulletin.

H.V. KALTENBORN

This is H.V. Kaltenborn, coming to you from Washington. It has just been learned that Germany and Russia have signed a mutual nonaggression pact in Moscow . . .

In the kitchen someone turned up the volume.

**KALTENBORN**

. . . and German Foreign Minister von Ribbentrop apparently guarantees that neither country will attack the other, should hostilities break out in Europe.

The two teenage girls had gone to the counter to pay their bills, but the proprietor's attention was focused on the radio broadcast.

**KALTENBORN**

There is jubilation in Berlin, but shock and grave concern in London, Paris and other world capitals. Most foreign observers feel that, with his eastern front secured by this treaty, Hitler is now free to pursue his offensive against Poland.

I thought about what Buck had said. But Great Britain and Germany were not going to get together—not against Russia, or anybody else; that possibility had now been eliminated.

**KALTENBORN**

It remains to be seen how Number 10 Downing Street will respond to this dramatically changed situation. But tonight the threat of war in Europe is very real. This is H.V. Kaltenborn, reporting from Washington.

**ANNOUNCER**

We now return you to the Goldbergs . . .

I sat there for a minute or so, then closed the magazine, and went over to pay my bill. The proprietor took the money and gave me my change, without saying anything. It was all very quiet, very still. I went outside, and started back toward the bus. The rain had stopped, but drops were still falling from the trees into the swollen gutters.

# XVIII

Everything was changed after that. It was like the difference between thinking you might have appendicitis and finding yourself being wheeled up to the operating room. There were a lot of new feelings crowding in on each other. Resignation. A sense of helplessness. Disbelief. A kind of weariness. Shock.

Yet, curiously, an impatience to get on with it; to make a start, so that one day there could be an end.

We talked about it a couple of nights later, a bunch of us. Buck was there, and Cotton, B.G., Sweetcorn, one or two more.

"It ain't got nothin' to do with us," Sweetcorn said, "nothin' atall, that I can see."

"You got it right," Cotton agreed. "Them silly bastards want to kill each other, let 'em go to it. The more, the better. Hell, they is all white, ain't they? No offense, Joe."

"Yeah, fuck 'em," B.G. put in.

"Might not be that easy," Buck said.

"What do you mean?"

"Saying you don't want in doesn't mean you can stay out."

"Aw, that's shit," Cotton said. "You been listenin' to Roosevelt, him and that damn dog. They's a big ocean out there, man."

"Not so big any more," Buck told him. "You hear 'bout a guy named Howard Hughes?"

"Huh?"

"Flew 'round the world, all the way 'round, in three days and somethin', a month or so back," Buck said.

"That don't mean nothin'," B.G. told him.

"I don't know," Sweetcorn said. "I hear they is flyin' every day now from out 'round New York someplace to Paris. Flies one way, they can fly the other."

"I don't care 'bout that," Cotton said. "It ain't our fight, I know that much."

We fell silent for a minute or so, then Buck turned to me.

"How about you, Joe?" he asked. "You think Canada will be in it?"

"I don't know," I said. "They usually do what England does, but I don't think they have to."

"You got the same king, though," Sweetcorn said.

"Well, yeah, in a way," I told him.

"Will they make you go?" Pete Simpson asked.

"Can't if he's down here," Cotton said.

"Maybe they send for him," Sweetcorn said.

"Sendin' ain't findin'," B.G. said.

"That's a fact."

B.G. snickered. "Don't know what it means, though," he said.

What would I do? It was the first time I had consciously thought about it.

"The generals and them people is runnin' it now," Cotton said.

"I got nothin' 'against no Germans," Pete said. "What they ever done to me?"

Sweetcorn got up and did a kind of flapping caricature of the Nazi goose step, as we had seen it in the newsreels. "Got some pretty good reams, though, ain't they?" he asked. "Look at me, I'se doin' it!" We all laughed.

"Joe?" Buck asked, after a minute.

"Have to wait and see, I guess," I told him.

"Stay the fuck out of it, that's all," Cotton said. "It ain't our fight."

"No damn way," B.G. added.

Malachi came along just then.

"Who's for some poker?" he asked. "Cotton, you in?"

"Yeah, I'll play," Cotton said.

"Joe?"

"Sure," I said.

We came to the last few days of August, then edged over into September. There was a touch of color in the trees—just a flash of yellow or red on a single limb here and there. A couple of times we saw football teams practicing, sweat running down the players' faces, because it was still hot. The corn and wheat rustled and waved in the lush, late-summer breezes. Newspapers advertised Back to School specials on kids' clothing and shoes. Field tomatoes were 5¢ a pound.

We played Illinois towns, one after the other—Galesburg, Peoria, Kankakee, Champaign. The same drifting-in crowds of town people and farmers. Lights on before

204

"Play ball!" Shadow. The reams. Laughter. Dust. The chatter. Sweetcorn's shrill voice, jabbering away. Once in a while the feel of a base hit tingling in my wrists. That good, old two-run margin, as sure as that B.G. would fart and Chappie smile. Always the bus.

Day by day the headlines in the newspapers were set in steadily larger type, and their portent grew ever more ominous, as the irreversible countdown continued in Europe.

Tuesday, August 29: *HITLER DELIVERS WAR ULTIMATUM TO POLAND*

Wednesday, August 30: *TIME RUNNING OUT IN EUROPE; ARMIES MASS*

Thursday, August 31: *BRITISH PEOPLE SET FOR WAR!*

Friday, September 1: *BLACKOUTS IN LONDON, PARIS; WORLD ON THE BRINK*

And, as I read the words and listened to people talking about what was happening, there was another new awareness—that I was already a long way from home.

# *XIX*

*Saturday, September 2, 1939.*

Decatur, Illinois.

That was the first day of the long Labor Day weekend and a carefree, holiday mood prevailed in spite of the gloomy news from overseas. I guess people had just said the hell with it. A lot of farm families were in for the day. One thing the kids knew for sure was that school would be starting come Tuesday morning.

The annual Central Illinois Exhibition was in full swing at the Fair Grounds. Rides. Sulky races, the horses snorting and lathered. Girlie show. Candy floss in paper cones. 4-H Clubs. Home baking and patchwork quilts and cakes and jars of done-down peaches. Toffee apples on sticks. Lost children, crying. Mustard. Bingo. A wheezing calliope.

Carnies. Shills.

"Tell ya what I'm gonna do . . ."

Raspy voiced barkers.

"Hey, c'mon in! See the lovely ladies, direct from the World's Fair in New York City. It's all here, on the inside. Hurry! Hurry! Hurry!"

The sights and sounds and smells.

The midway started just beyond the right field fence of the ball park. Buck, Luke and I went over there for a while in the early evening—me with the lampblack on, and the ball cap to hide my hair. The dry grass was trampled down and worn by hundreds of feet. The grasshoppers jumped dispiritedly among the empty popcorn cartons and other debris. There was a lot of dust in the air.

On the way back we stopped at a small tent, open on three sides, in which a short, wizened man in a cook's hat was presiding over a grill covered with sizzling chopped onions. We didn't know whether he'd serve us or not, but there wasn't any trouble.

"You fellas with the ball team?" he asked, as he flipped our hamburgs over in among the onions.

"Uh-huh," Buck told him.

"I seen you play once, back where I come from," he said.

"Oh, yeah? Where's that at?" Luke asked.

"Canada. Place called Three Rivers, up in Quebec. Maybe you been there."

"Yeah, I remember it," Luke told him. "Man, you is a long way from home."

"Not as far as a lot of others are gonna be, once the shooting starts."

"Looks like it's coming, all right," Buck said.

The little man was slicing a tomato with a long, sharp knife.

"Comin', hell," he said. "It's right on top of us."

There was a good crowd on hand that night, one of the best we had all summer. It was soft and warm, and the sky was filled with stars a million miles beyond the paltry halo of the lights. Infinitely closer, the midway was going strong. A nice night for a ball game.

From the first inning on, though, my attention was increasingly distracted by a girl in the right field stands. She was sitting alone, four or five rows back, and there was something about her that kept drawing my eyes like a magnet. Dark haired, slender, quietly dressed—interesting in an indefinable way.

And every time I glanced in her direction she was looking at me. In the fifth I went over near the stands to catch a high pop-up, and she was only about twenty feet away when our eyes met. It was strange. Her look was almost a stare, so steady and unblinking were the eyes; yet I saw neither rudeness nor boldness there, only a kind of open, straightforward frankness.

I was curious about her, but, more than that, I wanted very much to know what her voice sounded like and to hear her laughter. To know a little of what she thought about, cared about, was.

Unfortunately, the prospects were about the same as my chances of replacing Lou Gehrig as the first baseman for the New York Yankees. All kinds of schemes, ever wilder and more frantic as the innings passed, ran through my mind. None of them offered any hope. Maybe I could feign an injury. (Would she rush down from the stands and cradle my head in her arms while we waited for the ambulance?) Perhaps I could get a note to her somehow. (Dear Wide Eyes: Meet me at the Crown-and-Anchor Game. Joe.)

Then, unbelievably soon, it was the bottom of the ninth. We should really give the fans more for their money, I thought. Maybe the Decatur Dodgers would rally, tie it up, and send us into extra innings, allowing me more time to work something out.

The Decatur Dodgers?

Against Latimore Lee, when he could practically taste his after-the-game meal?

It was just zip—zip—zip, and all over in the ninth. Well, those last three batters would be able to tell their grandchildren that they'd seen—or not seen—a real fast-ball once in their lives.

The All Stars were running off the field, but I lingered behind, crouching down to tie a shoelace that hadn't come undone. Not ready to give up even then, I searched the stands desperately for a glimpse of the girl. The fans were filing out—kids, old ladies, fat men, preachers and school teachers, farmers and undertakers.

But not her; she was gone.

When I finally made myself accept that unhappy reality, I straightened up and walked slowly across the in-field and through the gate in the left field fence.

The others had gone on ahead, and I was all alone as I walked toward the bus.

I felt depressed, let down, as though I had lost something I'd never had.

And suddenly there she was in the circle of light under a lamp post. Just standing alone.

I stopped. Maybe half a minute went by, and then I

went toward her—she was a tall girl with a lithe, natural grace.

Standing a short distance apart, we looked at each other.

"You aren't black," she said.

That threw me, all right. Was she going to call the police, spit in my face—what?

There was no one within earshot. The fans were drifting away in other directions. Should I try to bluff it out? Or what?

I studied her face, searching for some sign. I should be able to see past those open eyes, I thought, and into her mind; but their exposed surface was of dark, smoky glass.

And there was something else. She was light skinned, but not quite white. Her forehead and high cheekbones were subtly tinted with sepia. Her nose, her lips, the blue-black of her hair—there was a little of Buck and Sweetcorn and Chappie there. Some part colored—maybe a quarter, a tenth, a fiftieth.

Did that make the situation better or worse?

"It's all right," she said. "Really. I didn't mean to embarrass you."

"How did you know?" I asked.

"You don't move quite the same," she said, "but mostly it's your face. Oh, and your eyes, of course."

"Blue, right?"

She nodded, smiling for the first time. "Yeah!"

"You're wondering what it's all about," I said. "Why I'm here."

The smile faded quickly.

"Oh, look," she said, "I'm sorry. It isn't any of my business."

"Don't worry about it."

"I was interested, that's all."

"It's kind of a long story."

"Sure, and you have to go with the others."

"Yeah, they'll be wondering what happened to me," I said. "I could meet you in a little while, though."

Her face brightened.

"Really? Do you want to?"

"Very much. I'll need about half an hour. Where will I look for you?"

She glanced over her shoulder.

"How about the Ferris wheel?"

"Does it know your name?" I asked her.

"No, but you could whisper it, if you like. It's Ellen —Ellen Marshall."

"That's nice."

"If you don't show up, who do I ask the FBI to look for?"

"Joe Giffen," I said.

She turned and was gone.

My mind raced ahead as I hurried back to the bus. Sunday was an open date, and we weren't scheduled to move on until the following day; so at least I didn't have to worry about cuttin' a hog on Chappie. But I had to get away on my own—and I had to do it without admitting that I had a date. With who? Couldn't be with a colored girl because I'd never get away with it. Couldn't be with a white girl because that would break the All Stars' First Commandment. How about a girl who looked white but had a little Negro blood.

When I got back the scene was the same as on any of fifty other nights—some of the players stretched out in their seats, others pulling off sweaty uniforms, Chappie getting out his books, Malachi trying to round up a poker game.

I went along the aisle, doing my best to look nonchalant. Woodrow glanced up as I went by his seat.

"Where you been?" he asked. "You trip over the foul line or somethin'?"

But he dropped it when I didn't answer, and nobody picked it up.

At the back of the bus I poured some water from a pail into the enamel basin we kept there, and used a lot of soap to wash away the lampblack. I had almost finished changing into street clothes when Buck called back to me. As usual, he was reading.

"You going for some food?"

What could I say?

"Uh—yeah."

"I'll come with you," he said, putting down his book, and glancing around. Then, realizing that I had switched back:

"Oh, sorry."

No way to eat together, a black and a white. I was relieved, but at the same time I didn't feel very good about it.

"Just wanted to get away from your ugly face," I said. "Nothing personal."

"Stick your head in the bucket one more time," he said.

It was not like Buck to ask any questions.

I finished dressing, then slipped out the Emergency door that was mainly used when somebody was a little late in answering Gabriel's call; once B.G. had come sprawling through there on his face when we were doing about thirty miles an hour.

I ran across a vacant field, slipped between a couple of tents, and hurried along the midway, my eyes on the Ferris wheel up ahead. It was getting on toward midnight, and the crowd had thinned out considerably.

When I got there she was sitting on a carnival packing case, licking an ice cream cone and holding a second in her other hand. She jumped down when she saw me, and came over.

"Here," she said, handing me the other cone. "It's a little runny."

"How did you know I'd get here right now?" I asked.

"I just felt you would," she said.

We walked that night—out of the Fair Grounds, to the main part of town, and then along quiet side streets. It was a warm night. Most of the houses were in darkness, but now and again we heard muffled voices from porches and verandahs.

We just strolled, taking our time, talking.

Learning a little about each other.

I told her how I came to be playing for the All Stars and about Chappie—enough to give her the general idea.

"Has it been O.K.?" she asked.

"Oh, sure," I said. "It was just a fluke, but I'm glad. For a lot of reasons, but mostly because they're so good."

"Sure—but you're no slouch, yourself."

"No, I hang on, that's all. Put nine Joe Giffens out there, and your team probably would have won tonight."

I didn't really believe that.

"My team is the Detroit Tigers."

213

"Oh," I said. Hank Greenberg, Charlie Gehringer, Mickey Cochrane, Tommy Bridges, Schoolboy Rowe. Yeah.

Detroit was her home town. She was just visiting Decatur to spend part of her vacation with her mother's sister, her only living relative. It had been pleasant but not very exciting, and it was almost over; she had to be back in time for work on Tuesday morning.

"What do you do back there?" I asked.

She shrugged. "Type, take shorthand. Nice people—dull job. Walk-around money, that's all."

We came finally to her aunt's place, a frame house, painted white, back of a picket fence with a gate. Nothing fancy, but nice.

She turned to face me.

"Thanks, Joe—I really enjoyed talking to you."

Thanks?

I didn't want to say good-bye, to have it end there by the picket fence.

"What are you doing tomorrow?"

Her eyes showed her surprise.

"Tomorrow? But you'll be gone, won't you?"

I shook my head. "Not until Monday. I've got the whole day."

She smiled, then was laughing.

A surprising girl.

"What's funny?" I asked her.

"Not funny, just nice. Glad, I guess. So *we* can have the whole day. I've got a serious question for you."

"Oh, oh."

"I have to know."

"All right, fire away," I said.

214

"How do you feel about picnics?"

Cold roast lamb; that wayward image, not consciously summoned, flickered briefly on the screen of my memory. A picnic my mother and father and I had had on a rocky, pine-crested island when I was a boy. I recalled nothing whatever of that day, except that we had eaten cold roast lamb. Why would I remember that?

"Well, it depends," I told her. "With or without potato salad?"

"Oh, with, of course."

"Then I feel very good about picnics," I said.

"Come by around noon, then—okay?"

"Okay," I said.

# XX

*Sunday, September 3, 1939.*

Everyone on the bus was still asleep the next morning when I was ready to leave; everyone except Chappie, who was studying a folded copy of the *St. Louis Sporting News*.

I waited for fifteen minutes, hoping that he'd decide to go outside for something, but no such luck.

The ever-lovin' Emergency door offered no escape that peaceful Sunday morning; Chappie would have heard me before I made the top step.

Nothing to do but try to brazen it out.

I was only about half way up the aisle when Chappie spoke; the eyes in the back of that man's head could look clean through a brick wall.

"Sure hot-footin' it early to-day," he said. "You pinch-hittin' for the Eggman this mo'nin'?"

"Haven't been to church in a long while," I said,

which was true enough. Not in about four years.

"Keep thinkin' I oughta go myself," Chappie said. "Don't never seem to make it, though, what with one thing and another."

"Well, you got a Bible there, anyway," I said, nodding toward his baseball paper.

He chuckled. "That's right enough. Ain't too much sin in it though, 'cept some of these battin' averages."

"Guess I'd better be getting along," I said.

"Yeah, well, maybe you could put in a word for me while you is there."

"I'll do that," I said. "Thought I might take in a movie later on."

"Sure, sure," he said. "Have yo'self a good day, now."

I went on to the front door and out into the morning sunshine.

Sorry, Chappie. Sorry, God.

Decatur was sleeping in that morning too. In the dozen or so blocks I saw only a handful of people: two elderly ladies, who looked as if they *were* going to church; a thin, shirtless man, trimming his hedge; and a boy delivering fat copies of the Sunday *New York Times.* I was able to catch just one word of the front page headline: *WAR.*

The sky was a clear, light blue. It would be hot later on, but the elm trees spread shade across the sidewalks, and there was a gentle breeze out of the southwest. Birds sang. Flower-beds were trim, and lush, and alive with color.

Like its neighbors, the white house belonging to Ellen's Aunt Jo was at rest, that spring's coat of paint glistening in the sunlight. Aspen leaves fluttered in the

217

breeze. The grass was thick and very green.

Since first opening my eyes that morning, I had been looking forward to seeing Ellen again. Now, as I opened the gate in the picket fence and went in along the walk, that sense of anticipation rounded first and dug in for extra bases.

I was about to knock when I heard her voice.

"Joe?"

"Hi. Where are you?"

"Over here."

She opened a screen door as I walked along the verandah.

"Come on in a minute. I'm just about ready."

The big, high-ceilinged kitchen was cool, and seemed dark after the brightness of the sun. There was a picnic basket on the table, to which Ellen added two or three last-minute items that she took out of the ice-box. Wearing a white blouse, with a light blue skirt and saddle-shoes, she looked tall and slender, somehow both crisp yet soft at the same time, and very attractive.

"Guess what," she said, as she closed the lid of the basket. "Something good."

"How many tries do I get?"

"Just one."

"Let's see. I got it—Bing Crosby is going to stop by and sing for us."

"That's pretty close," she said. "Actually, Bing is tied up and can't make it—but Aunt Jo did say we can have her car for the day."

"That's even better. Aunt Jo?"

"Short for Josephine," Ellen said. "She's gone to church."

We put the picnic basket in the rumble seat of the Model A Ford, and headed east, with Ellen behind the wheel. It was the first time I had seen a woman or girl drive a car, and she was good at it. I told her so.

She shrugged. "It isn't very hard. Don't forget about Amelia Earhart."

"Sure, but she didn't make it."

"Not the last time—nobody does. But she flew a lot of miles before that. Anyway, what about Wiley Post?"

"I was just kidding," I said.

She smiled. "I know. I was driving my daddy's old truck back in Louisiana when I was eleven, maybe twelve. Just seems natural to me."

And, sitting there beside her, Ellen seemed natural to me too. It was nice with the breeze coming through the open windows.

We drove eight or ten miles out of town, then turned off onto a dirt road that twisted and wound between walls of thick forest. A hen partridge nervously shooed her brood of fluffy chicks along in front of her, shepherding them into the underbrush with her wings. A little further on a whitetail deer watched us with wary eyes for a moment, then leaped gracefully over a fallen tree and was gone.

After about a half a mile we came to an open area, a kind of natural park, where the grass was lush and green. In the trough of the gentle valley there was a small river, its surface sparkling in the sun as it meandered along between clumps of willows, like a Sunday golfer patiently hacking his way toward the green.

"The Sangamon," Ellen said.

The water flowed quietly, and I suddenly knew for

219

sure that a thousand generations of Indians had come there to hunt and fish and camp and leave their broken bits of pottery in the roots of the grass.

"Beautiful," I said.

Ellen parked the Model A in the shade of a giant oak that had been there for a long time, though not nearly so long as the river, and we got out.

For the next several hours it was as if the outside world did not exist; we didn't see another soul as long as we were there. Utter peace, the only sounds, apart from our own, coming from the gurgling water, the fluttering leaves, the waving grass, the scolding chipmunks, the birds. A borrowed interlude, a time out of time.

For a while longer we were still a little tentative with each other—the hesitancy deriving not from any awkwardness between us, but precisely because we *did* seem to get along so easily, so naturally, so *comfortably*. Because it felt right. Neither of us had experienced anything quite like that before and so we were inclined to be cautious about our relationship, to ask questions of it. Who was she, and who was I, and how had it come about that we found ourselves alone together on the banks of that little river in Illinois?

But as the afternoon slipped away—first the minutes, then the hours—and we lay side-by-side in the warm sun, looking up at the cotton batting clouds that drifted across the pale blue of the sky, Ellen and I came gradually, almost lazily, to accept it. And eventually we spoke of many things.

Always, from as far back as she could remember, she had wanted to be a dancer. Any kind of dancing—tap, soft shoe, ballroom; in a Broadway musical or a night club act; as a star or as a member of the chorus line. But, above all, ballet. There had been a few lessons when her parents were still alive and able to scrape a couple of extra bucks together. Later, a Negro dance mistress who had driven her until her shoes ran red, screamed at her, loved her, believed in her. Afterwards, a few public appearances, and a handful of reviews that described her as "promising." Now, evening classes at a neighborhood Youth Center in her part of Detroit.

"Imagine me with a dancer," I said. "That's great."

She smiled, and shook her head. "No. Pretty good, maybe, but a long way from great."

"It's never too late," I told her.

"Joe, let's always be honest with each other, shall we?"

"Okay, sure."

"It was too late by the time I was twelve. If you don't have it then, you never will."

Like me and good curve balls, breaking off sharply just in front of the plate. A pretty fair fastball hitter against semi-pro throwers, that was all.

I told her about that, and she understood, partly because her uncle had made her into a Detroit Tiger fan.

We described to each other what it was like growing up in Natchitoches, Louisiana, and Trentville, Ontario. Our parents, our homes, our schools, our friends.

At one point we started to talk about color, about her Negro grandfather and about Chappie and me and the All Stars, but soon found that we couldn't stay serious on that subject for very long—at least not then, there by the river.

"The way I look at it," I said, "we're both both."

"Either that," Ellen said, feigning deep contemplation, "or neither neither."

"Let's see now, you're mostly one, but partly the other —right?"

"Uh-huh. You, though, you're a hundred percent this way or that way."

"Except when I don't get it all off," I told her, running my hand over my face.

"That happens, eh?" she asked, biting her lip.

"Oh, yeah."

"My, it certainly is complicated."

"Well, color isn't just a simple matter of black and white, you know," I said, barely able to get the words out.

We gave up after that, and laughed until tears came to our eyes.

"Oh, Joe."

I leaned over on my elbow then, bent my head down and we kissed for the first time. Her lips, surprised but hesitantly responsive, were warm and honest and tasted faintly of salt from a tear of laughter. Our mouths separated, came together again three or four times, saying things for which we had not yet formulated any words.

We lay in each other's arms for what seemed like either a moment or an eternity, and then Ellen pushed me gently away and sat up.

"I think," she said, "that it's time for a swim."

"The old cold shower treatment?" I asked, half jokingly.

Ellen nodded. "Yes—for me."

"One trouble," I said, "I didn't bring a suit. Mostly because I haven't got one."

222

"Then we'll just have to have some rules," she said. "That will be your part of the river, down there, the other side of that pine tree. I'll stay up here, to the left of those rocks. Okay?"

"It's a deal," I said, noting somewhat ruefully that the tree and the rocks were about thirty feet apart, which seemed like a pretty wide neutral zone.

We got up, and I went down-river a little piece, where I stripped off my clothes behind a clump of alders. Then, feeling somewhat self-conscious, I made my way to the river and quickly waded in. The water was cool, but not cold as I pushed off and began to swim, looking upstream for Ellen. To my surprise she was already in, swimming easily, her long hair damp in places, a couple of loose strands drifting languidly on the surface.

"Hi!" she shouted. "Nice, eh?"

"It's warmer down here," I called back.

"I'll take your word for it."

We enjoyed the river for ten minutes or so, splashing, laughing. A couple of times I cheated a bit on the pine tree, and once or twice she drifted down past the rocks, but mostly we played by her rules.

"What do you think?" she called, finally. "Getting hungry?"

"Starving!"

"Me too!"

I drifted in to the bank and waited there, wanting to make sure she was out of sight before leaving the water to get my clothes. That's how I came to know that she too had gone in without a swim suit. I saw her for just a moment, from a considerable distance; but it was long enough, and near enough, to take my breath away. Tall,

223

lithe, beautiful; a tanned, dancer's body.

She smiled when I joined her, looking up from the picnic she was spreading on a white table cloth.

"I didn't have one either," she said. "It's back in Detroit."

We ate cold chicken, ham, potato salad, tomatoes, deviled eggs, corn bread, apple pie with cheese. There was a big thermos of iced tea, which was still cold. All very good.

By the time we were finished, the shadows had spread over us and reached the near bank of the river, as the late summer evening rapidly closed in. It was noticeably cooler too. On a game night we would have been getting ready to take our cuts in the top of the first inning. A whippoorwill began to call from somewhere far off, and about ten million mosquitoes came out of the cedar thickets and tall grass. They were as hungry as we had been an hour earlier.

It was Ellen's idea that we take in a movie. Neither of us knew what was on, but it didn't matter; we were just looking for a way to spend a few more hours together before we had to say good-bye, an inevitability that was always there, always with us, that day.

I helped her pack up what was left of our picnic and we got into the Model A and headed back for town, frantically rolling up the windows to shut out as many as we could of the humming hordes of insects.

When we drove into Decatur, it was practically dark, and the lights were coming on—in the windows of houses, in the neon signs along the main street, around the marquee outside the Regent Theatre: *Love Finds Andy Hardy* with MICKEY ROONEY, JUDY GARLAND & LANA TURNER.

Ellen parked the car and we joined a few other couples who were buying thirty-five cent tickets. The theatre was only about half full and we found seats on the aisle near the back. About thirty seconds later my hand found Ellen's, and held it for the rest of the show.

Fox Movietone News, with the smoothly dramatic voice of Lowell Thomas. Tragic floods in India. Prime Minister Neville Chamberlain arriving at Number 10 Downing Street. Billy Rose's "Aquacade" at the New York World's Fair. Then a mammoth military rally in Berlin, with dozens of rumbling tanks, hundreds of artillery pieces, and thousands upon thousands of goose-stepping Nazi soldiers.

All too soon the lights came up in the theatre, and we were out in the full night. It was quite a bit cooler by then, cool enough to make a fastball really sting if you caught it in tight on the handle of the bat. We got into the Model A to drive the five or six blocks to her aunt's place and suddenly there was an overpowering awareness that our day was fast coming to an end.

Ellen parked the car in the short driveway between the trees, and we went around and sat on the steps of the verandah in the shadows. Aunt Jo had apparently gone to bed; there was a light on upstairs, and the sound of a radio drifted down to us from an open window.

We talked in low voices, re-sharing some of the moments of our twenty-four hours . . . laughed softly . . . touched . . . kissed.

The hands of unseen clocks moved on toward midnight. Coming up Monday.

"What time is your bus?"

She sighed. "Too early to think about."

"Too damn soon to think about too," I said.

225

"I know. How about you, when do you go?"

"If I know Chappie, he'll have us out of here first thing," I said.

She smiled. "Don't you mean 'Mr. Johnson'?"

"Not when he insists on leaving at the crack of dawn," I said. "Then it's just plain old 'Chappie'."

Upstairs the music had given way to a news broadcast. The announcer's voice sounded weary, as if he had been on the job for a long time that holiday Sunday.

German troops and armored units were pouring across the frontier into Poland. Warsaw was in flames. French armies were massing along the Maginot Line.

And then: "There have been several air raid alarms in London, but so far no enemy planes have been reported over the city. . . ."

Over London?

Then the announcer confirmed what most people had known for hours—since about the time Ellen and I had set out in the Model A. The final British ultimatum. The German rejection. The somber declaration.

Great Britain was at war with Germany.

Of course the Field Marshalls and Admirals couldn't have been expected to divert their timetables for a picnic or an Andy Hardy movie.

Beside me, Ellen shivered.

"Oh, God," she said, "it's come."

"I guess so."

We stood up spontaneously and she came into my arms.

"Not an easy way to find out," she whispered, "or a good time."

"No."

226

Could it ever be easy or good?

A sob passed through her body.

"I don't understand," she said, her face close to mine. "All of a sudden everything seems to be ending. The summer is over . . . the world we knew . . . even my vacation . . . you and I. Why, Joe, why does it all have to be over?"

"I don't know," I said. "Maybe it just seems that way, right now. Who can tell? Maybe there'll still be some time."

Her fingers tightened around my arms, digging in, wanting to remember for both of us. We kissed once more, and the salt in her tears that last time owed nothing to laughter.

"It's too much," she said, "too much for right now. You take care of yourself. Maybe another time . . . we'll see."

Then she turned and was gone, the screen door closing slowly behind her.

After that there was just the cool night, and the mottled, empty shadows, and the radio, which had gone back to dance music.

I stood there for a long moment, then went along the path and through the gate in the white picket fence.

# XXI

*Monday, September 4, 1939.*

I didn't get much sleep that night—nor, I'm sure, did a great many others in a wide variety of places and circumstances. Frightened people. Bewildered people. Lost people. Conscripted clerks and plumbers and farmers' sons who had killed other men that day. Those who wept for the world. Excited Staff Officers, pouring over their battle charts. Intoxicated heroes. Wives. Mothers. The already wounded, in their pain and loneliness.

Around me, everything was reassuringly familiar, normal. Sweetcorn over there, with the covers pulled up over his head as always. Chappie curled up nearby, such a frail little bundle of bones. B.G. snoring away. Gabriel waiting.

I was warm and comfortable enough in the nest of bedding I had bought with my first pay, away back in Brandon, Manitoba, at the beginning of July.

My eyelids were heavy and my body yearned for rest, oblivion.

But there were too many things running across the stage of my mind, and the curtain was off its track.

I tossed and turned for a long time, then gave up at last and lay with my hands behind my head, looking up at the stars.

There was the war, of course, the reality of it now, permeating everything. All around, in the coolness of the night, lurking there, faceless as yet, but waiting to step forward in its own good time.

What would it look like, smell like, sound like, be like?

How do you go about saying hello to war?

That terrible stranger.

I had read the newspapers, and listened to the radio whenever I could, but I had no idea what war was about, no understanding of how it had ultimately come to be inevitable, no grasp of whatever principles might be involved, no feeling of any personal involvement. None of it made any sense to me. How could an old, worn-out Englishman push his sagging face up to a microphone and, just by saying some words, commit millions to death and dismemberment? Did that make it so? And the people I had known—none of whom had ever had very much—what difference did it make to them if Germany invaded Poland?

Were they—was Joe Giffen—really at war?

What for?

I thought about those pot-bellied veterans of the Great War, the medals clanking on the lapels of their blue serge suits, standing there in the cold rain by the cenotaph in Trentville on those November mornings when the bugler played "The Last Post." Hell, they would have been young then, back in 1915 and 1916, and couldn't have known what it was all about either. Of course. But I had never thought of that before.

"It ain't got nothin' to do with us," Sweetcorn had said. And he was right. Nothing. Not a damned thing. Not with me, or with anyone I had ever known.

"Stay the fuck out of it," Cotton had said. And that was good advice.

And yet . . .

Suppose you get trapped in a burning building. Maybe you just happened to go there at the wrong time. Maybe you should have noticed the place was a fire-trap before you went in. Maybe the landlord was cheating on his tenants. Maybe the Safety Inspector was slipped a few bucks to overlook faulty wiring. Maybe there weren't enough emergency exits. Maybe some newspaper reporter should have exposed the situation.

Maybe a lot of things.

But by the time the flames are shooting up the stairwells and the dense smoke is charring your lungs, none of that matters. Too late then, what could have been or should have been. Irrelevant. Academic. History.

When it comes there are only two things you can do: look for a way out or stay and help to fight the fire.

I thought about my father, who had read so much more than I had about wars and what causes them. Had that led to a greater understanding for him? He had tried to enlist during his war, my mother had told me once, but been rejected because of ingrown toenails. Was that plausible? It was a foot soldier's war, all right—but couldn't the medics have corrected that condition? Had he found his way out?

Not much help there.

I remembered what Ellen had said, about everything ending. It was true. The summer. The Thirties, even though they had four months left to run. The Great Depression. Two decades of peace.

Certainly, the summer. The calendar might give it another two or three weeks, but Labor Day was back-to-school, close-up-the-cottage, put-away-bathing-suits time. From then on it would be football and fall fairs and falling leaves.

I had been putting off thinking about that, but it couldn't wait much longer. The All Stars were already beginning the annual migration that would eventually take them away down into Central America. The next day we were scheduled to make a big jump to Paducah, Kentucky. Not long after that would come Tennessee, Alabama, Georgia, Mississippi, Louisiana.

And there was just no way that a white first baseman from Trentville, Canada, was going to pass as colored down there in the Deep South. No way.

My time with the ball club—that too was fast running out.

Had Chappie given that any consideration? I smiled to myself; you could bet he had.

At last the sky began to grow a little lighter in the east, first the false dawn, then a tinge of pink laced with streaks of yellow and orange. While it was still dark on the earth a light came on in the window of a house across the street from the Fair Grounds, and I thought about Ellen again. She would probably be getting up about then, her Aunt Jo perhaps making breakfast for her in the kitchen. Another hour or so, and she'd be on her way back to Detroit. I wondered how she felt, and if I was in her thoughts, and whether I would ever see her again.

Daylight chased the last dark soldiers of the night over the far horizon and our little camp gradually came to life. Buck, as always one of the first up, slipped away and returned a few minutes later with a morning newspaper. The headline said that the Cunard liner *Athenia* had been torpedoed and sunk off the coast of Ireland, with heavy loss of life. The rest of the paper was almost all war news, all of it pretty confusing.

Back on page five I found a short, wire service item, datelined Ottawa. The Canadian government, it said, had pledged unlimited support to Great Britain, while temporarily reserving judgment as to the extent and nature of its participation. It also said that there wouldn't be any compulsory military service "at least in the foreseeable future."

By ten o'clock that morning Malachi was behind the wheel of the bus, and we were on our way to Springfield, Illinois, some forty miles away. I took a few minutes to think it through one more time, and then went up the aisle and stopped at Chappie's seat.

"Mr. Johnson?"

He turned from looking out the window.

"Yeah, yeah, Joe. Sit down here. How you gettin' on?"

"Not so good."

"Oh? You ailin' some way?"

"Not that. Just seems about time I was moving on."

He nodded. "Uh-huh, kinda figured that might be it."

I told him about some of the things that had been going through my mind.

232

"Well, you right 'bout the South," he said when I finished. "Wouldn't want you to go tryin' it down there. Hard enough when you is the real thing."

I laughed a little with him.

"This war, now," he went on, "it changes things—oh, my, it does! We gonna be in it too, sooner or later. I ain't got no doubt 'long those lines. Start gas rationin', all that stuff. Won't pay much mind to no little-bitty nigger ball club, don't seem likely."

Then he brightened, smiled. "Hell, that ain't your worry, though—ain't nobody's yet, come to that. You be headin' no'th, then?"

"I guess so."

"What you gonna do back there? Join up—that what yo' thinkin'?"

"Don't know," I told him. "I haven't got that far." There was just the feeling that it was time to go home, to be home. I couldn't explain why, or what good I thought it would do. It certainly didn't come from any sense of duty or patriotism. Nothing like that. Truthfully, I both mistrusted and resented the feeling. But it was there.

"How soon do you want to get away?" Chappie asked.

"Well, the more south we go, the farther I'll have to come back," I said. "Depends on when you can get somebody else in. I won't leave you shorthanded, though."

"I'll make some calls, soon as we hit Springfield," he said. "Damn, I don't guess I'll ever get used to it."

"What?" I asked him.

"Losin' one of my players."

One of his All Stars.

"I won't ever forget this summer," I said.

"Well, you done your share," he said. "Get along now. I gotta look up some phone numbers."

"Thanks, Mr. Johnson."

We got into Springfield around noon, and before sup-pertime Chappie had made arrangements to bring in a replacement.

"Charlie Lloyd," he told me, "from down Louisville. Played some with the Kansas City Monarchs, and the Pittsburg Crawfords. Good barnstormer, from what I hear. Gonna meet us tomorrow night in Paducah."

So, that was that.

By game time that night the others knew I was leaving, but nobody said anything about it. It was almost as if I was already gone, and that bothered me some; not that I expected anybody to break out in tears or make speeches, but, after all, I'd been around, a part of them, for more than two months.

Well, I thought, first basemen come and first basemen leave, but the All Stars go on forever.

It was a warm night, almost like mid-summer except for the early darkness, and there was a good crowd on hand. A thousand, maybe. We went through the famil-iar, pre-game routines, finishing up with shadow ball, and it was just like every other night, all the way back to Alcona, Manitoba.

Except that it was the last time.

Then the plate umpire got things under way, and the innings passed quickly, one after the other. We got a run in the second on Pete Simpson's drag bunt and B.G.'s triple to deep center, then added another in the fourth when Buck hit one halfway to Chicago.

"You ready for 'ain't lookin'?" Chappie asked me, as

we were getting ready to go out for their half of the fifth.

"Sure," I told him. One thing—if Malachi missed that once, the army wouldn't want me.

We took the field, and a couple of minutes later I rolled the practice ball in toward our dugout, after tossing the usual warm-up grounders to the other infielders. Then, as Luke Redding got ready to pitch to their first batter, it was time to go into my act. I turned my back on the diamond, and stared at some imaginary phenomenon in the night sky just above the rim of the right field stands.

Their first base coach was the first to turn around to see what I was looking at, but soon gave up with a shrug: who could figure out what might catch the fancy of a nigger ball player?

As always, the fans soon picked it up. What the hell was I doing? What was out there? Didn't I know there was a game going on? Hoots. Guffaws. Derision. The wisecracks never varied from town to town.

That's all right, I thought; my turn is coming. And they were really set up for it too. I hadn't heard a crowd respond like this all summer.

In 'ain't lookin' ' I could usually pretty well keep track of what was going on behind me by interpreting the familiar sounds of the game—the slap of the ball into B.G.'s mitt, the ump's 'Ball' and 'Strike' calls, Sweetcorn's constant jabbering. But in all the noise that night, I was afraid I might not hear the crack of the bat—my signal to start counting. And, if my glove wasn't there when the ball arrived—crunch! The nerves began dancing in the small of my back.

What were we waiting for anyway? Luke Redding was doing the pitching, and he could get a grounder down

235

the third base side just about any time he wanted. And the fans didn't need any more warming up; they were already going crazy as it was. So, come on.

Another minute went by . . . two . . . and still nothing happened; and because I was beginning to feel foolish, I let my eyes drop a little so that I could see the people in the first base stands. They were all standing up, laughing. It was a good-natured, contagious laughter. They were really enjoying themselves.

And all of them, every last one, seemed to be looking at me. Hell, I thought, this isn't that funny.

Come on, Luke; let's do it, man!

Still—nothing.

I stuck it out as long as I could, for maybe another sixty seconds, and then I just had to turn around.

The field was completely deserted.

No infielders. No outfielders. No pitcher or catcher. No batter. No umpires.

Nobody.

Just me.

Then the fans really began to laugh. At first I was so embarrassed that I just wanted crawl under the bag and hide. But gradually I began to appreciate the beauty, the perfection of it, and I started to laugh too. What a ream!

The All Stars emerged from the dugout, first Sweetcorn, then the others, and formed up along the third base line, clapping and whistling.

The plate umpire came out, took off his cap, and made a sweeping bow in my direction.

I decided that it was time to get out of there, and the fans gave me a standing ovation as I trotted off the field. You would have thought I had just hit a home run to win the seventh game of the World Series. When I got to the sidelines Chappie shook my hand and the others swarmed around, slapping me on the back.

Things gradually subsided after that, and a few minutes later they got the game started again.

In the dugout I looked along the bench, studying each face in turn for a sign of guilt.

"All right," I demanded, "who did it?"

No answer.

"You, Malachi?"

His expression was as innocent as it would ever be.

"Uh-uh, not me," he said.

"Sweetcorn?"

The shortstop shook his head in exaggerated fashion.

"No sir," he said. "I woulda done it if I hadda, but I never."

"Well, somebody did," I said.

Then B.G. began pointing surreptitiously, and some of the others picked it up. Their fingers all converged on one man—Chappie.

He was standing with one foot up on the dugout steps, leaning on his knee with his elbows.

I had to follow it through.

"Mr. Johnson?"

"Not now, Joe," he said over his shoulder. "Not while I is managin'."

That killed us. Managing—the All Stars?

"Shhh," Sweetcorn said, "he thinkin' up some strategy. Gonna use a pinch hitter, maybe."

"Ain't nobody not playin'," Woodrow Wilson Jones said, " 'cept Latimore."

"Better get his seein' eye dog loosened up, then,"

Sweetcorn said. "Make him blink his eyes a time or two."

"Who, Latimore?"

"Hell, no, the dog."

I couldn't see Chappie's face, but his thin shoulders were shaking with barely controlled laughter. Finally he turned around.

"Tell you one thing," he said, not looking at anyone in particular, "that ream is retired, as of tonight."

There was still the rest of the ball game to finish. Luke let up a little to let the home team score its token run in the seventh, and it was still 2–1 for us when we came to bat in the top of the ninth.

Sweetcorn hit a lazy fly to their left fielder for one out, bringing me to the plate. Chappie was in front of the dugout, leaning on one knee, and he waved me over.

"I'd be obliged if you'd get me another run," he said. "We ain't got but one on them, and you can't never tell what'll happen in a ball game."

"I'll try," I told him.

"Guy they got out there," Chappie said, "likes to throw two fast ones, then curve ya. Ain't got much on it. You notice that?"

"He does hang one every so often," I said, though I hadn't detected any particular pattern.

"Uh-huh, well see if I'm right," Chappie said.

I went up to bat, shuffled my feet around until they felt comfortable, and stared out at the pitcher. A big, raw-boned, Corn Belt kid—strong, but without much control. Just a thrower, really.

His first pitch was a fast ball, low and away.

His second was another hummer that caught the inside corner for a strike, according to the umpire.

If Chappie was right, the next pitch should be a breaking ball.

It was.

It hung.

About as big as a dinner plate.

I smiled to myself; you shouldn't have done that, country boy. Not with an All Star.

Then the bat came through the ball, and it was out of there in the first fifteen feet.

A real downtowner.

I was most of the way to first when the ball sailed over the fence on a collision course with the moon.

Their left fielder went back until he ran out of ball park, then peered in toward the mound, as if to say: "Don't look at me—I didn't float it up there. And I ain't got wings."

That was my first home run of the summer, and it narrowed the gap between B.G. and me in that department to about thirty-nine.

The fans gave me a hand as I circled the bases, probably figuring that they owed it to me after inning number five.

Chappie and the others shook my hand or slapped me on the back when I returned to the bench.

All Stars 3, Springfield Stars 1.

It ended that way about ten minutes later, when I took a looping throw from Sweetcorn for the final out.

I straightened up, the ball cradled in the webbing of my glove. Time to head for the barn.

It hit me just as I was passing the third base chalk-line, taking care not to step on it, as all responsible, superstitious ballplayers—black and white—always do.

And at the same moment the rest of it came flooding back too. The war. Ellen. Other things.

A lot of past, present and future.

My knees felt weak for a few steps, until I got control of it. You have to.

We took down the lights, put the bats and balls in the bags, packed up, ready to move on to the next town.

Then we went for a meal at a place Chappie knew, an all-night diner run by a black guy who had played for a while with the Cincinatti Clowns. Good food. Pork chops, ham and eggs, home-fried potatoes, grits, black-eyed peas, all kinds of pie. Eat yourself to death for half a buck.

An hour or so later Buck and I talked in low voices, as we had so many times that summer, across the aisle of the bus. He told me the whole story of the great 'ain't lookin' ' ream.

It had been Chappie's doing, allright.

"Figured it out way back—before shadow, even," Buck said. "Let everybody in on it, 'cept you, of course."

This is what had taken place behind my back, while I was staring off into the empty night sky:

Acting on Chappie's instructions, Luke had struck out the home team on nine, rapid-fire smoke signals. Zip—zip—zip, times three. The Gawk could probably have retired any trio of hitters in the world like that, if he had a mind to. Or a chance to.

Then, with the inning officially over, Chappie had directed the rest of it, waving everybody else in, one or two at a time, so that I couldn't see what was happening out of the corner of my eye. First, the All Stars. Then the other team and the men-in-blue.

Until there was nobody left out there, except Joe Giffen, looking the other way—at nothing.

Beautiful.

A classic.

"He was sure enough managing then," I said.

Buck smiled, nodded.

"We all promised not to let on," he said, "but I kind of figured you'd like to know."

# XXII

As usual, the Eggman came through the next morning, thereby maintaining his average for the summer at .1000.

When I woke up there was a fire going, and Stumpy Simpson's one hand was darting back and forth like a humming bird as he cracked sunny-side-uppers into the two big frying pans.

We ate breakfast when it was ready, and then I went to the bus to get my gear together. Chappie had suggested that they drop me off at the main north-south highway, which they would cross about ten miles down the line on their way to Paducah.

He was working on his account books when I got there, but he didn't look up as I went past on my way to the back. There wasn't much to it, once I found my khaki dunnage bag, which had been collecting dust in a corner

242

of the luggage rack since the end of June. Just my clothes to pack, mostly the same ones I'd arrived with, shaving stuff, a few other odds and ends. I'd be travelling light again, so I decided to leave the ground sheet and blankets for Charlie Lloyd, in case he needed them. The nights would be getting cool from then on, even further south.

Then I folded the pants and shirt of my uniform, laid the cap and stockings on top, and took the small pile up to Chappie. The mending job he'd done after Clyde Everett's spikes ripped into my leg was holding up pretty well.

"Guess you'll be needing these," I said.

"Yeah, well just put it here anywheres," he said. "You know, you took hold o' that one pretty good last night. Your daddy woulda liked to see it, I do believe."

"Well, you set it up for me," I said.

"Wasn't the onliest time you was set up," he said, a twinkle in his deep-set eyes.

"No," I said, "and both times by one of the best in the business."

"Don't rightly know what you mean there," he said, looking perplexed. "I is too old to fool with that kinda stuff."

"How have you been feeling?" I asked him.

"Huh?"

"You know," I said, nodding toward his chest.

"Oh, that," he said. "You ain't said nothin', has you?"

"No."

"That's good," he said, " 'cause it ain't riled up none since that last time. Oh, we'll keep goin' long as we can . . . long as they let us."

"Yeah, well you take care of yourself," I told him.

"Oh, I always does that," he said.

Sure—by eating greasy food at midnight, sleeping on the hard ground, chasing fly balls when you are fifty-four years old.

Just then Woodrow got on the bus. It was his turn to drive.

"You ready to go?" he asked Chappie.

"S'pose so," he said, looking at his gold pocket watch. "It comin' up ten o'clock."

Woodrow leaned on the button, sounding Gabriel's horn, and a minute later the others came trooping in. No "hog-cutters." Typically, B.G. was the last to come on board, and about halfway down the aisle he turned his huge ass and let go a real boomer.

"Aw, shit," Cotton said, reaching hurriedly to open his window as far as it would go.

"Not quite," B.G. said. "That the secret of it, man."

We left Springfield behind, and headed east along a secondary, blacktop highway. Most of the corn was in by then, and red and green combines were taking off the lightly coppered wheat, one long strip after another. The farmers would be looking up at the overcast sky, praying for the rain to hold off—just for a few hours, after all the days and weeks. Would we have a game that night?

No, not 'we'—they.

About twenty minutes went by, and then Woodrow called back to me.

"Look like we comin' up to it now."

I pick up my few belongings, and made my way forward.

We said our good-byes, each in his own way.

"Be good, now."

"I'll try, Little Cool."

244

"Keep loose, you hear?"

"As a goose, man."

"So long for now."

"Yeah, be seein' you, Cap."

"All the best, Gawk."

"You, too."

When I got to Chappie's seat, he was standing up and holding out his hand. I took it. The thin, still so strong fingers.

"Thanks for everything," I said.

"We'll run 'cross you somewheres, the Stars and me," he said. "It ain't that big a world."

"Sure."

"This war, now," he said, "don't go swingin' at no bad pitches."

I smiled. "What if I don't see anything I like?"

"Take a walk, then. Ain't nothin' wrong with that."

"Beats striking out," I said.

"Oh, yeah, every time."

I nodded, squeezed his hand once more, and turned away. We were at the intersection by then and Woodrow made the turn south and then pulled off onto the shoulder, throwing open the door with the driver's handle as we came to a stop. I stepped down, went along beside the bus, and cut across behind it to the opposite side of the highway.

We were finished with words by then, but I waved good-bye to Buck, who was driving the truck that morning.

A moment later Gabriel waddled back out onto the oil-stained cement, to the familiar grind of changing gears.

I watched the two vehicles, looking after them until

they crested a hill a mile or so away. It seemed likely that they would reappear, growing smaller, at least once, but they didn't.

When I was sure that the hill had hidden them for good, I began walking north along the dusty margin between the weeds and the gravel.

About a mile farther on a stream ran under the road, between the weathered cement pillars of a small bridge. I scrambled down the steep bank, stripped off my shirt, and scrubbed my hands, arms, face and neck with a bar of soap. Then I rinsed, scrubbed again, rinsed again. The last traces of lampblack were discernible only a few feet before being dissipated by the gentle current.

Back on the highway, and white again, I started to work my thumb. With two or three good hitches I might make the Canadian border by early evening. That would be where Detroit looks across the St. Clair River to Windsor, Ontario, and I had already decided to spend a little time with Ellen before going the rest of the way home.

After that? Well, the Motor City was only a few hours from Trentville by train or bus. Before too long I should be able to get a few days off from whatever job I found . . . or a short leave from the army.

The army?

Clanking medals, 'The Last Post,' long dead comrades. Long dead.

Don't worry, Chappie, I thought. I won't get suckered up at the plate. Maybe I'll take four. But sometimes you have to hit away. Keep the pitcher honest. Establish that you aren't about to be intimidated. Get on with the game. You know these things better than anybody else.

Count the customers.

As I walked along, the kit bag over my shoulder swung lightly against the 'ain't lookin' ' hollow in the small of my back. I thought of the first base mitt in there and wondered where and when I'd get to use it again.

F
~~08356~~
CR/7

Craig, John

Chappie and me

| DATE | | | |
|---|---|---|---|
| A pr.27 | | | |
| May 27 | | | |
| 1·22-01 | | | |
| 2/1/01 | | | |
| | | | |
| | | | |
| | | | |
| | | | |
| | | | |
| | | | |
| | | | |